SPECIAL MESSAGE TO READERS

THE ULVERSCROFT FOUNDATION
(registered UK charity number 264873)

was established in 1972 to provide funds for research, diagnosis and treatment of eye diseases. Examples of major projects funded by the Ulverscroft Foundation are:-

- The Children's Eye Unit at Moorfields Eye Hospital, London
- The Ulverscroft Children's Eye Unit at Great Ormond Street Hospital for Sick Children
- Funding research into eye diseases and treatment at the Department of Ophthalmology, University of Leicester
- The Ulverscroft Vision Research Group, Institute of Child Health
- Twin operating theatres at the Western Ophthalmic Hospital, London
- The Chair of Ophthalmology at the Royal Australian College of Ophthalmologists

You can help further the work of the Foundation by making a donation or leaving a legacy. Every contribution is gratefully received. If you would like to help support the Foundation or require further information, please contact:

THE ULVERSCROFT FOUNDATION
The Green, Bradgate Road, Anstey
Leicester LE7 7FU, England
Tel: (0116) 236 4325

website: www.foundation.ulverscroft.com

SPRING AT TAIGH FALLON

When Angel Tempest finds out that her best friend Zac has inherited a Scottish mansion from his great-aunt, she immediately offers to visit Taigh Fallon with him. It will mean closing up her jet jewellery shop in Whitby for a few days, but the prospect of a spring trip to the Scottish Highlands is too tempting. Then Kyle, Zac's estranged and slightly grumpy Canadian cousin, turns up unexpectedly at Taigh Fallon, and events take a strange turn as the long-kept secrets of the old house begin to reveal themselves . . .

KIRSTY FERRY

SPRING AT TAIGH FALLON

Complete and Unabridged

LINFORD
Leicester

First published in Great Britain in 2019 by
Choc Lit Limited
Surrey

First Linford Edition
published 2020
by arrangement with
Choc Lit Limited
Surrey

A catalogue record for this book is available
from the British Library.

ISBN 978–1–4448–4396–5

Published by
F. A. Thorpe (Publishing)
Anstey, Leicestershire

Set by Words & Graphics Ltd.
Anstey, Leicestershire
Printed and bound in Great Britain by
T. J. International Ltd., Padstow, Cornwall

This book is printed on acid-free paper

And moving thro' a mirror clear
That hangs before her all the year,
Shadows of the world appear . . .

Extract from *The Lady of Shalott,*
Alfred, Lord Tennyson.

Dedication

To Shaun and James, with an extra 'thank you' for my beautiful Whitby jet necklace.

Acknowledgements

Welcome to the eccentric and quirky world of the wonderful Angel Tempest. She's the youngest of my three fictitious Tempest sisters, and you may already have met Rosa, the eldest sister, in *Summer at Carrick Park*.

Angel's fabulous workshop is entirely influenced by The Ebor Jetworks in Church Street, Whitby, North Yorkshire. Should you ever go to Whitby, please take a few moments to squeeze into this splendid little shop and try to imagine Angel working there, just on the right as you walk in. I have a beautiful jet necklace from Ebor, and I love it. If you are down that way, you might also like to visit the Whitby Museum in Pannett Park, and see some incredible examples of traditional jet jewellery from the nineteenth century.

Angel, from the very moment she

appeared in my imagination, just had to be a rather gorgeous Goth, and I hope her personality endears her to you. She was quite a strong lady and leant herself well to a fresh take on the traditional Gothic stories many people love to read.

In order to bring Angel's lacy, Victorian-inspired character to life, I have to thank my wonderful publishers Choc Lit, my fabulous editor and super-talented cover designer.

I'd also like to thank the Choc Lit Tasting Panel for their faith in the story (particularly Marlies B, Alison G, Katie P, Lizzy D, Isabella T, Vanessa O, Caroline U and Carol F who passed the original manuscript and made publication possible), our wider Choc Lit family of very special authors, and above all, my truly supportive family and friends. They are the ones who have put up with the grumbles and self-doubt as I wrote this story — as usual! Thank you so much. I love you all.

Prologue

'My angel,' he murmured, reaching his fingertips out to her. They touched cold glass and she was still there, behind it, watching him. He would welcome her when she finally came.

This was not the first time he had seen her, not at all. He had seen her before, seen this dark angel, with the strange markings on her skin and the black eyes that matched his own . . .

1

Angel Tempest. It was a name that really should have been in lights. Instead, it was painted in white lettering on a black wooden sign that creaked back and forth over the doorway of a jet workshop in Whitby.

Angel Tempest herself huddled inside the shop, polishing bits of the black fossilised wood that washed up on the North Yorkshire coast until they were luminescent. When she had drawn all the possible beauty out of each precious facet, she would set the newly created gems aside until she decided what to do with them. Some of the jet would adorn heavy silver lockets; some would end up in rings; some would end up in brooches or tiny boxes or as simply small pebble shapes that people loved to touch and hold.

'The jet tells you what to do with it,'

Angel was fond of saying. 'I never know myself what it'll turn into until it speaks to me.'

'Hello, Angel.'

Angel looked up from her work as a little girl, around about six years old, pushed through the doorway and stood in front of Angel's battered wooden table.

'Good morning, Grace,' said Angel. Grace's father, Jon, owned the photography studio opposite Angel's workshop, and Grace had grown up surrounded by the Victorian gothic splendour of the town. Whitby was famous, after all, for Dracula, Goth weekend and reams and reams of black lace, taffeta and pale, vampiric faces. Which was probably why Grace simply studied Angel curiously and raised a small, chubby finger tipped with a bright pink varnished nail to point only centimetres away from Angel's nose.

'That's a pretty one,' she said.

'What, this?' asked Angel, pointing to her diamond nose-stud. 'Thank you. Zac sent me it.'

'I like Zac. Are you going to marry Zac?'

Angel dipped her head to her work and smiled. 'No, Grace. Zac's just a friend.'

'Hmm,' replied the little girl. Since she had been a bridesmaid the previous Christmas, she was keen to repeat the honour. 'I do think you'd look pretty in a wedding dress. Elodie was beautiful in her white dress.'

'I don't really do white dresses,' replied Angel.

'You could probably have a black one,' suggested Grace. Then she sighed, lustily. 'I don't think Aunt Lissy and Uncle Stef will get married.'

'They might surprise you. Has Aunt Lissy been visiting? Your nails are very pretty.'

Grace inspected the nail varnish. 'Yes. I wanted black but Mummy said no.'

'Maybe when you're a bigger girl.' Angel grinned at the child.

'You always have black nails.'

'I have black everything. But I'm a bit older than you.'

Grace nodded. She blinked her curiously coloured eyes, one blue, one green, identical to her father's and her aunt's, and took a step closer. 'What's that going to be?'

'It might go in a necklace.' Angel held out the oval gem she was working on. 'Do you think?'

'You'll have to see what it tells you.'

'Indeed I will. Here — you can have this little bit.' Angel picked up a broken piece of jet that hadn't really obliged her in the polishing process. 'You can keep it safe.'

'Thank you!' Grace took the gem and pocketed it carefully. 'Oh — I know I had to ask you something. We're going to the tea shop and Mummy said to ask if you want some coffee.'

'Well that would be lovely. Tell your mummy thank you.'

Grace nodded and headed out of the shop. Angel saw a figure hovering around the door and she smiled knowing Becky, Grace's mother, would be waiting outside with Grace's tiny new brother, Charlie, in his pram, ready to collect her daughter and walk around to the tea shop. The street was narrow and cobbled between the two properties and Grace was used to running in and out of them — but the tea shop she referred to was a short walk away and Angel knew Grace wouldn't be allowed that far on her own just yet — even if her attitude was sometimes that of a person much older than six.

★   ★   ★

It wasn't long before Grace came back, gripping a cardboard tray very carefully. The tray held a cup of coffee in one part and a half-eaten chocolate cookie in the other compartment.

'I'm very sorry, Angel, but that's my cookie,' Grace informed her. 'I had nowhere to put it.'

'That's fine. Thank you for the coffee.'

'You're welcome,' said Grace. Angel leaned across her workstation and took the tray from Grace, waiting until the child had reclaimed her cookie before wiggling the cup out of the holder and placing it next to her.

'I do like that dress.' Grace wandered over to a dummy in the corner of the workshop which was draped in a black Victorian mourning gown. She reached out and fingered a ruffle on the sleeve, before realising, it seemed, that she wasn't supposed to touch it and pulling her hand away.

'Yes, it's lovely, isn't it?' Angel had long ago decided not to go into the fact that the dress hardly represented joy and partying, as the little girl liked to imagine. After all, the black costumes that filled Whitby were all beautiful and everyone seemed to be having a lovely time; there was no reason for Grace to associate black with death and mourning.

'It's very like your dress.' Grace turned and smiled at Angel. Her bottom two teeth were missing, Angel noticed.

'Almost like mine.' Today, Angel was wearing a tightly laced bodice, a long, full black lace skirt, a black velvet choker and chunky black boots. She flipped her long, black hair over her shoulder and cast another glance at the mourning dress. It was awfully pretty, despite the fact, Angel knew, it was a maternity dress. Desperately sad — and absolutely no need to go into that one for Grace, either.

Grace's eyes drifted covetously up the rickety wooden stairs to the jumble of storerooms and attics above the workshop. Angel knew she was determined to get up there and poke around, considering there was a cosy flat above her father's photography studio — but this was very much a workspace for Angel and she had no desire to share the attics as living space with the mice that scampered around up there. She resolved to get herself a cat at some point.

The bell above the door rang and

Becky poked her head through.

Becky smiled at Angel, then called for her daughter. 'Come on, Gracie. Leave Angel to do her job.'

Grace sighed again and turned, pouting, to Becky. 'All right,' she said. 'But I was just *looking*.'

'Hmmm,' replied Becky. 'You look with your eyes, not your fingers. I bet you've been touching things again.'

Grace pulled a face and turned to Angel, ignoring Becky. 'Goodbye Angel. I'll see you soon. I'm not back at school for almost two weeks.' She held up two fingers as if to drive home her point. 'After the Easter Bunny comes.'

'It'll be a long two weeks for your mummy,' replied Angel wryly.

'It won't be too bad. Lissy's coming back again next week.' Becky held her hand out and smiled. 'She can amuse her for a couple of days. I don't think she can cope with Charlie as well, though — Jon and I will deal with him ourselves. I don't want to put Lissy off coming to see us.'

Grace took Becky's hand reluctantly and allowed herself to be led out of the shop. The child turned and waved solemnly at Angel then the door shut behind them. Angel shook her head and laughed, turning back to her jet.

She had decided the piece she was working on was ideal for a pendant, and was just about to fashion a setting for it when her mobile rang. 'Zac! Hey there!' She smiled into the receiver.

'Angel?'

Zac's voice was unsteady and Angel frowned. 'Are you all right? You sound a bit . . . weird.'

'No,' said Zac, in his soft, Scottish accent. 'I'm not all right. I've just inherited a house.'

'A *house*?' Angel stared at the mobile. 'Who from?'

'My great aunt.' The line was remarkably clear for once, ringing as he was from the Isle of Skye. Zac lived in a renovated croft, making heather gems and polished Cairngorm stones into jewellery. It didn't matter, he said, that

11

the Cairngorms were in the east of Scotland and he was to the west — it was how he fashioned the stones that mattered. He and Angel had met years ago at university and, after one drunken, fumbled attempt at sleeping together, in a grotty flat Angel's older sister Rosa had briefly lived in, had decided they were better off as friends. It worked much better for them.

'Is that the one who used to come and see you? I'm sorry.' Angel looked up as a couple of customers walked into the shop and headed purposefully towards the cabinets at the back of the room. Angel recognised them as having been into the shop earlier — they'd obviously decided what they wanted to buy now. She turned her attention back to the phone call.

'Yes. Jeanie. She'd always come to us, really. I haven't been to her house since I was little. I remember one time I went, she was all dressed in black like Poe's raven — no offence.' She imagined him pushing his too long, mousey-brown hair off his face and wondered if it had grown any longer since the last time she saw him — it had been chin-length then, but he didn't seem to see the necessity in cutting it.

'No offence taken. But seriously?' Angel said, opening her black-rimmed eyes wide.

'Seriously,' said Zac, the sound of papers rustling carrying down the line. 'As I grew older, I got to know her better, and she was lovely really. I remember we used to meet up with some other family members at her house when I was very young, but they lived abroad and didn't come home very often. I remember playing with an older cousin. He was called Kyle and he was a bit of a pain. He thought he was ten times better than me because he was older, and I thought he had a loud voice and a weird accent. He tore the head off my Action Man once. And he wouldn't let me read any of the good books Aunt Jeanie had. Told me I was too little and put them on a shelf out of my reach. But as I got older, Jeanie would come and visit us, on her way to Edinburgh or York or London. She used to enjoy travelling. Anyway, I just got this letter and beside the fact I'm still reeling that she's dead, it's talking about some old, convoluted inheritance where the house gets divided between the members of the youngest generation.' There was a more furious rustle. 'Which means I get some and if they find anyone else, for example my cousin, they'll get a share too. I can't quite believe that she wanted anyone like us to have the place!'

He sounded puzzled and Angel found that amusing. 'If they find anyone else? You mean like a random relative they dredge up? Or, as they say, your cousin. Who, incidentally, sounds vile.'

'Aye. Mam thinks they're still in Canada. All she ever heard was family hearsay though.'

'As if anyone from Canada is going to be interested in an old-lady house.' Angel watched the customers point to something and nod at each other, as if they'd finally settled on a purchase. 'Look. I've got to go, I've got some customers. I'll call you later, okay?'

'Okay. Talk later.'

'Bye, for now.'

'Bye, hen!' Zac disconnected the call. Angel grinned as she tucked the phone into a drawer and then removed the little set of keys that would open the cabinet for the customers. Hen. Zac was truly distracted. He hadn't called her 'hen' ever.

★ ★ ★

Zac looked at the stiff, official letter from the solicitors and frowned. An old-lady house was the last thing he wanted.

He'd taken years to set up his little business and now he'd had one of the barns converted into a cosy tea room. The building next door to that was his workshop and, quickly finding that the more remote parts of Skye had very few places for coffee, he picked up quite a lot of passing trade from people leaving Armadale, where the Mallaig ferry dropped them off. It was also a useful place to have a gift shop for his jewellery — people were either highly excited to be on Skye or sad they were leaving, so they wanted souvenirs.

Ivy McFarlane, from the village of Broadford, about twenty minutes away, had made herself beyond useful by helping out in the tea room; but despite the fact his tea room would be well looked after, Zac was reluctant to go to the mainland — as always — even for a short time.

Best case scenario was that they couldn't find any other relatives, or his cousin just said 'forget it'; if so, he'd just instruct someone to sell the place. He looked out of his window at the Cuillin Mountains looming up blackly across the moors.

The mainland. Nope. Not his scene at all.

★   ★   ★

In Ontario, however, Kyle Fallon was opening up a similar letter.

'What the hell?' He looked at the letter and re-read it, scowling. Scotland. Land of his forefathers. The place he'd been named for. He'd been over here all his life. What the hell did he want an old-lady house for? It wasn't the way he'd planned out his future. No. His life was here, and he intended to remain here.

Kyle leaned back in his chair and crumpled the letter up. He tossed it towards the bin. Inheritance or no inheritance, he wasn't interested. There would have to be, he considered, something pretty special to entice him over there. And to keep him over there.

Scotland.

Bleak. Cold. Misty.

Ugh.

He stared at the wastepaper bin. He'd missed the damn thing, and the paper was lying beside it. He swore to himself, and got out of the chair, fully intending to properly discard it this time. There was a key as well, a big, old-fashioned one. He supposed he'd better send that back, to be honest.

Okay. Yeah. He should probably retrieve the address and get the key sent back . . .

But as he leaned down to pick it up, something stopped him.

Maybe it was the name of the place — Taigh Fallon. Maybe it was the idea of the place — it did look pretty interesting, and as a property developer he had an eye for that sort of thing. He remembered visits when he was a kid to Great Aunt Jeanie's, and wondered if the place would be as vast and as creepy as he'd remembered.

Or maybe, just maybe, it was something that flashed into his mind; a memory from so long ago, he wondered exactly where it had come from. It didn't seem to be a conscious memory of the Taigh Fallon he recalled. It was a room. A room in a tower. And a mirror.

And the memory of a dream that

seemed to have haunted him all of his life.

Taigh Fallon. He picked the paper up and smoothed it out.

Maybe he wouldn't toss the letter into the trash just yet. Maybe he needed to think more about it all, than just jumping on the fact that he needed to send the key back.

2

Angel locked up the workshop and walked through town, heading down the narrow streets towards the bridge.

Continuing onwards, she walked along the road until she came to a small alley-way that led her into a tiny courtyard edged with cottages. Angel's was the end cottage, a cheerful white-washed, blue-doored house that had probably once belonged to a fisherman. There was just enough room at the back to house Angel's car, which was pulled up right against the window.

She unlocked the front door and was straight into her lounge. She tossed her bag on the sofa and then made a beeline for the kettle. The cottage was a quirky little place, set over three floors, the entire top floor given over to a single room. Even now, after five years, Angel was unsure whether it should be a bedroom or a lounge. It was nice to think of turning it into a proper living area — but then, she reasoned, she'd be two spiral staircases away from the kitchen and that could be dangerous if she was carrying anything hot.

So for now, it was just The Room, and more for storage than anything else. Her flounciest dresses and most elaborately boned and laced corsets hung from a wooden clothes rail in there, and portfolios of her work, along with advertising leaflets and catalogues and business cards she hadn't taken down to the shop yet, lived on the floor, stacked up in piles for her to deal with at some point. Her luggage, too, was there — old battered travelling trunks and a more modern suitcase and holdall if she needed them, along with an old sewing machine and a lot of Victoriana that she had decided was too nice to display in the shop.

Angel might look as if she had stepped out of a nineteenth-century portrait, but she was quite a modern, practical person in most ways. She went to her handbag and picked up her mobile and texted Zac, telling him she was now home if he wanted to call her.

Within a couple of minutes, the mobile rang, the ringtone blending disharmoniously with the whistling of the now-boiling kettle.

'Zachary Fallon! Or must I call you Sir, now you've inherited property?'

Zac made a disparaging noise and took up the lament of being a beneficiary of his great aunt's generosity once more. 'I've Google-mapped it,' he said. 'It's definitely on the mainland, and it's not an old-lady house. It's bigger than I remember it; it's truly a mansion thing, Ange.' He pronounced it 'Aynge'.

'A mansion thing?' Angel was intrigued. She poured boiling water onto some instant coffee and stirred the liquid, inhaling the strong, delicious scent as she did so. She took her coffee black and carried the cup a couple of steps across the room, settling herself on the over-stuffed sofa with the phone still pressed against her ear.

'Yes. It's in the Western Highlands, near Loch Long and the Falls of Glomach — I think it's near Eilean Donan castle.' The Scottish words rolled off Zac's tongue delightfully.

'I love Eilean Donan,' mused Angel, taking a sip of her drink. 'Very atmospheric.'

'Yes, yes,' said Zac, with the attitude of someone who had heard that phrase a million times. 'And you hate Glencoe because you reckon it's still haunted with memories of the massacre hundreds of years ago. I know all of that. Ange — what I don't know, is what I should *do*. They've even sent me a key! This big old iron thing that looks as if it should unlock a mausoleum.'

The answer was obvious to Angel. 'Go there,' she said simply. 'Go and see what it's like properly, with you being an adult now and all that.'

'But I don't *want* to go there. I've got more than enough going on here to see to.'

She imagined him tossing the key down in front of him in disgust. 'You sound like a spoilt brat, Zac. Can't Ivy manage for a week or so?'

'Why should she? It's *my* business.'

'And I'm sure she's more than capable of selling cakes and making coffee and showing people your beautiful jewellery. Look, it's April, I know you're busy, but there are bound to be bitey insects on Skye. There always is, in my experience. Escape them — go to the old-lady house!'

'The midges aren't confined to Skye, you know? They'll be on the mainland too.'

'You should still go.' Angel's eyes drifted around her small lounge and settled on the black, wrought iron spiral staircase. Up *there*, was her luggage. She looked out of the back window. Out *there* was her car. She hadn't had a holiday for months. 'I'll come with you, if you like,' she heard herself saying.

There was a brief pause. 'You'd come?' asked Zac.

'Yes. I guess I would.' Angel grinned at the staircase. The idea of a week in the Western Highlands was suddenly very, very appealing.

'But who'll look after your workshop?'

'The workshop can look after itself. I suspect Grace Nelson would like to run it, but as she's only six, I think I'll just lock it up for a week. No harm done. It's not really peak holiday season yet, and Goth weekend is at the end of the month, so we're fine. Jessie might pop in to check it over if I ask her, but I'm not bothered.' Jessie — or Jessamine, to give Angel's sister her full title — owned a second-hand book shop in Staithes, a higgledy-piggledy fishing village a few miles north of Whitby. Staithes was the haunt of many a geologist and the sisters shared a mutual love of jet.

Rosa, their oldest sister had always been deemed the more sensible of the three of them, and she worked at Carrick Park Hotel on the moors near Whitby. Rosa grudgingly liked jet, but was much happier with discreet, small pieces of jewellery which complimented her immaculate style. Like pearl earrings and neat little necklaces. Try as she might, Angel couldn't really imagine Rosa with jet jewellery at all.

There was another silence from Zac as he apparently contemplated the way forward. 'You think I should go, then?' Angel imagined him frowning and puzzling over the answer.

'For goodness sake!' Angel was exasperated. 'Yes. Look — give me the weekend, then I'll set off Sunday evening. I'll stop off in Edinburgh, and come up to Skye Monday. Or I can meet you at the old-lady house. It's up to you.'

'Come to Skye first.' Zac sounded a little relieved. 'You can see what I've done to the place since last time.'

'No problem. You sure you're okay with this before I come? You'll not decide to hole up in your croft and not bother?'

She heard Zac sigh. 'No, you're right.

It needs to be done. I owe it to the old girl, I suppose. But I don't want to be staying there overnight. I don't like the mainland.'

'You do owe it to Jeanie to go. And you are very silly about the mainland. We don't all bite, you know. Not as much as your horrid Island midges do, anyway. Right, I'm going to sort my packing out. I'll see you Monday, and I'll have my usual room, yes? You haven't messed *that* one up too much with your renovations, have you?'

'Of course not. And anyway, it's far too pokey for a normal human being to sleep in. I can't do anything sensible with it. See you Monday. And thanks.'

'I'm only coming because I'm nosey,' said Angel with a smile.

'I know.'

* * *

Angel was glad to realise that Zac's voice had an answering smile in it as well. The plane ride was uncomfortable and too long. He'd managed to get some tickets pretty quickly, and he shouldn't complain as it was business class, but still. He could have done without the hassle. Someone tried to engage him in conversation — a girl, fully intending to backpack from Land's End to John o'Groats. Or the other way around. Kyle Fallon wasn't really sure. He smiled automatically and answered her questions very vaguely, and was conscious of that old iron key in his hand luggage.

The girl chattered excitedly, her conversation spattered with 'like', and 'kind of' far too frequently for his liking. He assumed that, as she was business class too, she'd decided to set off in style; either that, or she had a rich Daddy who was indulging her whims. At some point, Kyle closed his eyes and drifted off into a daydream where he was in a circular room, lined with bookshelves. And there was someone else there. A girl who he felt he should know. Then he touched one of the bookshelves and —

'So hey. We should hook up. If *you're* going to Scotland and I am as well, it can't be *that* big a place, can it?' She smiled widely at him, her teeth too white and too perfect against her tanned skin and her bleached hair. Perhaps Daddy was a dentist? It was a thought.

'Yeah. Maybe we'll see each other around.' He smiled and tried not to sound too much as if he meant it, although she wasn't paying much attention to anything except the sound of her own voice.

He didn't really want to see her. The girl who had drifted into his dreams of that weird circular room was a million miles removed from this blonde girl.

The girl who he had glimpsed was dark-haired and dark-eyed, and the idea of her gave him chills along his spine. But he couldn't see her face very clearly, and dammit, that was driving him *kind of* crazy.

3

Skye was as beautiful as ever. Angel had travelled up to Mallaig and took the 'back door' in, as she liked to call it, right into Armadale and straight up the new coast road, all the way to Zac's croft. She grinned as she recalled Grace's face, when she informed Becky and Jon she wouldn't be around for a few days.

'Will the old house be haunted?' the child had asked, her mouth forming a perfect 'O' at the prospect.

'Maybe.'

'Do you think you will like the ghosts?' Grace had pressed.

'I don't know. If they're nice ghosts, then yes.'

'Do you think you will be brave enough to stay with them?'

'I think I will be, yes. The dead can't hurt you, so I'm not worried.'

'Promise you will *try* to stay with them?' Grace had asked. 'Because they might be lonely.'

'That's enough, Gracie,' Becky had said, warningly. 'The house will be perfectly lovely and won't have any ghosts.'

'But — '

'I promise I'll try to stay with them,' Angel had said quickly.

'That's good,' Grace had said, nodding sagely.

That child was a tonic, as Angel's gran used to say.

She was still smiling at the memory when she approached Zac's croft. It wasn't hard to miss it — a discreet sign made out of polished onyx hung at the end of the lane which led into Zac's piece of land. He had converted the croft so instead of being a small two-roomed building, it now had an upstairs with three bedrooms and a bathroom, and a nice glassed over conservatory at the back, which more or less doubled the size of the place

31

— although it wasn't obvious from the front. The conservatory gave a good view of the jagged Cuillins, about fifteen miles to the west. Angel had been here once when a storm had swept in; she knew it was one of the most spectacular things she would ever witness, with the clouds rolling over the island, punctuated by bursts of lightning, claps of thunder and the biggest raindrops she had ever seen.

The front of the croft, whitewashed and slate-roofed, still looked very traditional. The two stone built barns to the left of the house were home to Zac's tea room and workshop. Behind those, way across the fields, was a derelict croft that was on Zac's land, but not worth doing anything with, in his opinion.

Angel loved it all, always had done. It was also a tonic to be up here and to see Zac again. He wasn't in the habit of coming to Whitby very often, which was a crying shame.

She'd hoped things would change

and he'd have more time to visit, because he'd recently employed a girl called Ivy McFarlane to work in the tea room. Ivy was, apparently, an artist and was also renting a place in the village nearby. She had, Zac told Angel, been experimenting with some gemstone and crystal jewellery to sell in his gift shop and by all accounts she was enjoying it, although she was perhaps going to move to Glastonbury at some point.

'She's baking cakes for the tea room as well,' he'd said with a frown. 'Not quite sure what I'll do about that one when she leaves.'

And when Angel pulled up in front of the tea room and walked inside to introduce herself and ask where her friend was, she had liked Ivy on sight — a fair-haired girl, with laughing green eyes, she had immediately made Angel smile and complimented her on her jewellery, which was always a way into Angel's good books. She could see how the girl would do well somewhere like Glastonbury.

But, even more pleasant than the wild Skye countryside and the welcome Ivy and Zac gave her, was the underfloor heating Zac had recently installed in the croft. It was a boon, no doubt about it.

Beautiful though Skye was, it was bloody cold when Angel woke up the next morning, cocooned as she was in her usual room; a little, white-painted room that had a wonderful view of the sea.

The Sound of Sleat was grey and wreathed with a mist that drifted in on the tide, and Angel watched it for a while, wrapped in a patchwork blanket that was folded up neatly on the window seat of her room. She had opened the window last night to enjoy the mingled scent of the sea and the moors as she drifted off to sleep, fortified by fish and chips and red wine and a couple of drams of whisky.

Sitting by an open window quite naked had seemed a good idea first thing, but the damp was creeping in around Angel's shoulders now and she could smell the coffee, drifting up from the kitchen below her. Underfloor heating and a hot shower would be awesome — then a quick breakfast . . . she sniffed again. Bacon, sausage, eggs and fried bread, if she wasn't mistaken. Okay, maybe not such a quick breakfast, but a delicious one anyway — then they could set off.

Zac was still determined to drive back to Skye each night. He wasn't convinced he would need to do much to his great aunt's house. He had checked about power and water and all the practical things — because Zac was a practical sort of person. He said there was even a housekeeping agency involved to get it all nice and clean for their anticipated arrival.

'We can at least make a cuppa,' he had told her, 'and have a bath. And have clean sheets on the beds. Well — you can. If you stay there.'

Which reminded her she needed to make a move. Angel stood up and stretched, pulling the blanket more firmly around her before she shuffled off to the bathroom. She felt that the fact the power and everything was on would make it much easier to stay over for a couple of nights — she had never been fond of roughing it anyway — but Zac was stubborn.

Still, she resolved, as she dropped the blanket onto the warm, tiled floor and stepped into the shower, she and Zac weren't joined at the hip. She had brought with her the battered old carpet bag from The Room and, like Mary Poppins, could fit all she needed into there for a couple of nights at the old-lady house. She would be doing Zac's great aunt a favour, surely, making sure the place was looked after and lived in for just a little longer.

★   ★   ★

Kyle had landed in Aberdeen, on the last leg of his journey.

God. It was damn cold.

The sooner he got this business sorted and was on his way back home, the better. But part of him, when he wasn't taking much notice about it, told him he'd want to stay just a little bit longer . . .

It was all very weird.

4

'Is this it, then?' Angel craned forward in the passenger seat of Zac's battered old 4×4 as they pulled up outside a fairly large house at the end of a gravelled drive.

On the other side of the house, Angel knew, was a set of steps that led down through a wooded glen to the water-side. Across that water, were the ruins of Eilean Donan Castle. Angel loved the place already.

'It is according to the satnav and Google Maps.' Zac, stopped the engine. He leaned across and picked up a bundle of papers, looking at a photo-graph the solicitor had kindly provided him with. 'Certainly looks like the picture on here as well. I can't believe I've forgotten so much. I was only small when we used to come, though. I never used to take much notice.'

Angel nodded and looked at the place through the rain-spattered glass. It was grey-coloured stone and built in a kind of L-shape. The front door was part of a square porch that nestled in the centre of the two legs of the 'L' and there was a turret room to the side, topped with a one of the cone-shaped roofs that Angel always found fascinating in this part of Scotland.

'I adore it,' she said, her gaze taking in the sweeping gardens and the bay windows. 'I can't wait to get inside. Did your great aunt live here a long time?'

Zac nodded and rustled the papers together. 'Great Aunt Jeanie. Let's give the poor woman her proper name. Jeanie's father was born here, apparently, and it stayed in the family through that side. So Jeanie's father is my great grandpa.' He continued the family history. 'Jeanie's father was an only child and there was nobody to split the property up with; and as I understand it, Jeanie was the youngest child from his marriage. My grandfather was her older brother, but only by a couple of years. He always said they thought he would be their last, so if *he* was a surprise to them, I wonder what exactly Jeanie was.' He grinned. 'Maybe that's why she left the house to the younger generation. It must have been frustrating being the little one and getting hand-me-downs.'

'I can understand that.' Angel too was the youngest child. 'Only by the time the clothes got through Rosa and Jessie I quite often got new ones. Jessie was always ripping her stuff, climbing up trees and then falling out of them.' She smiled at the memory.

'I don't believe it. The photos you showed me of you when you were little make you all look very innocent.'

'Those two, maybe. Blonde and blue-eyed. Then there was me. I started off blonde, then my hair just got darker and darker.' She laughed. 'That's why they called me Angel, you know. Because I looked like one — to start with.'

Zac cast her a look that took in her

black hair, black choker and long, black dress. She was also wearing a jet mourning ring, in honour of Jeanie.

'You don't any more. I can't ever imagine you blonde.' He gazed at her critically. 'Maybe with a red tint in your hair, or a bit of plum going on. But never blonde.'

Angel flicked her long, soft ringlets over her shoulder and smiled. 'This is mostly natural, you know.'

'Mostly?'

'Mostly. Anyway. Let's stop talking about me and get into that place.' She pointed to the house. 'I hope you've got the key.'

Zac produced it from a jiffy bag and stuffed the papers inside the envelope instead. 'Here you go.'

Angel held out her hand eagerly and Zac dropped the key into her palm. He was right, it did look like a mausoleum key. Angel couldn't help but smile as she felt the weight of it.

'Perfect. Now — do you want to unlock the house, or can I?'

'As you're clutching the key like you'll never let it go, I think you might do me serious injury if I say I want to unlock it,' said Zac. 'Aye. Go ahead, love. Have fun.'

'Thank you!' She hugged Zac across the gear stick and opened the door. 'Oh — does it have a name?' she asked. 'The house?'

'Taigh Fallon. It just means Fallon House. The Taigh bit is Gaelic.'

'Taigh Fallon.' Angel mused on the words. 'Sounds nice, doesn't it?'

Zac peered out of the window and she hid a smile as he wrinkled his nose at, apparently, the grey sky and thick clouds, with the mist swathing the tops of the trees in the glen. 'Sounds nice,' he conceded. 'Not sure about *looks* nice.'

'This is no worse than Skye. Now, are you coming?'

'I suppose so.'

'Great. Oh — can you bring my carpet bag, please?' She grinned at his bemused stare. 'It's in the boot. With my overnight gear in it.'

'You really brought it?' Zac was incredulous.

'Of course I did. Come on. How long have you known me?' She paused, half-in half-out of the car. 'Would I ever pass up a chance like this? Look!' She gestured to the foreboding building which was shadowed now across the porch. 'How could I turn my back on Taigh Fallon when I've only just seen it?'

Zac shook his head. 'I'm not going to answer those questions because I don't think you really want me to answer them. All I will say is you're welcome to stay if you wish, but I won't be here.'

'And since when have I ever needed you to protect me? I'm a big girl. I *live* in a haunted house — '

'No you don't.'

'I live in a *potentially* haunted house. And it doesn't bother me. This is just a bit bigger. And I've never stayed overnight in a house like this before.' She took in the turret and slate roof.

'You can't deny me the chance, because that's like denying Grace Nelson a good story for when I return. And if you're selling this house, I might not get the chance again. And you'll be coming in with me now, at least — and if you still decide to go home tonight, then you'll be back tomorrow. So it's all good.'

'Angel!' Zac began, despairingly. Then he clamped his lips shut and shook his head. 'Forget it. Open up. I'll get your bag.'

'Thank you, darling,' she said, and finally slid out of the vehicle. 'Get yours as well. I made one up for you, just in case.'

1897, Taigh Fallon

The key turned smoothly in the lock, shutting out the world beyond Taigh Fallon. Waves shushed and rolled, shushed and rolled, breaking onto the rocky shore at the bottom of the steps, the sound muted but ever-present.

'Now we are assured that nobody will disturb us.' Annis looked up at Alasdair. Her hair was deep auburn, lit from behind with the flickering light of the candles, highlights of bright, spun gold tracing through her curls. The black gown did not become her. Already pale, her eyes haunted, the dark taffeta drew every last rose from her cheeks.

Alasdair frowned. 'But what reason do you have to lock the door?'

'I have every reason,' replied Annis. 'And I have dismissed the servants early tonight.'

Alasdair took in his sister-in-law, standing before him. Someone must have let the dress out again, but her growing stomach was once more straining against the taffeta, pulling the fabric ever tighter.

As if she felt his gaze on her, she laid her hand on her abdomen protectively. 'He would want me to do this,' she said. 'He would want me to.'

5

'Have you *seen* this place?' Angel stood in the hallway, her arms dropped at her side, her head turning this way and that, trying, it seemed, to see everything all at once.

Zac thought that, given a covering of feathers, Angel would genuinely have passed as an owl.

'360 degrees,' he muttered. 'If your head swivels 360 degrees, I'm calling an exorcist.'

Angel turned, the hem of her dress swishing against the polished floorboards. She glared at him. 'Funny boy,' she said, witheringly. She gestured around the hallway, pointing to the sweeping, oak staircase that seemed to double back on itself as it climbed through the house. 'You can't tell me you don't find this impressive.'

The hallway, panelled in matching

oak, was, to Zac's eyes, gloomy. And the old, tartan sofa in front of the fireplace there just seemed incongruous. There was, he noticed, another long wooden seat in an inglenook and an identical seat on the other side of the fireplace.

'I don't know if impressive is the word.' He dropped Angel's carpet bag on the sofa and moved towards a radiator, disguised by further panelling. He felt it, rather stupidly, he realised, and shivered. 'We need to find the boiler and get this place aired out and heated up. I can't believe it's April. It's so cold in here.' The sky was glowering at him beyond the stained glass windows, either side of the fireplace.

Angel, however, had moved across to the grate and was in the process of laying logs and kindling down. 'We can get this set easily,' she said. 'It'll give us some heat. It'll be lovely.' She stood up and wiped her hands on her skirt. 'I just need some firelighters and some matches, and if this was my place, I'd have them just about . . . here.' She lifted the seat of one of the wooden benches and revealed a storage area with a pile of neatly stacked firelighter blocks and a few boxes of matches. 'Marvellous.' She hunkered down and within seconds had a flame licking at the wood. It caught with a little *whoosh* and the fire began to burn brightly, throwing a semi-circle of heat out which would reach the tartan sofa before very long.

Angel grasped a poker from a fire-set and prodded the flames, making them leap a little higher. 'Hmm. I suppose we should have checked the chimney. Made sure it wasn't blocked.' She surveyed the fire for a couple of minutes, until, satisfied that they weren't going to choke on any smoke, she nodded and turned back to Zac. 'Do you know where the boiler is then?'

He shook his head. 'It'll be in the paperwork, no doubt.' He pulled the documents out of the jiffy bag again and rifled through them. 'Here. It's upstairs. In a cupboard on the landing.' He turned and looked at the stairs.

They too were highly polished oak, blending into the oak floorboards in the hallway.

'Awesome.' Angel flashed a quick smile at him and rushed past, heading towards the stairs, her boots thudding across the floor and echoing around the room.

'Be my guest,' said Zac, sarcastically.

'Of course,' Angel shouted over her shoulder, the sarcasm lost on her. 'I don't know which room is the cupboard, so — ' She thudded up the first few stairs and leaned over the banister at the first turning. ' — I'll just have to check them *all*!'

'You could use this floorplan!' cried Zac, uselessly. 'The estate agent drew it up — '

Angel was already out of sight and on the first floor. Doors opened and closed, then she shrieked with what Zac could only describe as unadulterated joy.

'There's another staircase — two in fact. One goes up to the attics, and another one comes up through . . . *this* room.' Her voice was faint. 'I wonder where it comes out downstairs? Hang on. Oh. The boiler. I've got the boiler, Zac.' There was a muffled clunk as something, somewhere kicked in, followed by a faint gurgling as water started moving through the pipes. Footsteps hurried along the landing and Zac watched the oak staircase for Angel sweeping down them. Instead, a noise from the room next to him startled him and he spun around.

'Well, hello.' Angel grinned, materialising next to him. 'The other staircase comes down into that room.' She pointed. 'I have to get into those attics, Zac. The house is like a bigger version of my cottage. Imagine the Taigh Fallon version of The Room.'

'I'd rather not. And you can't tell me you still want to stay here tonight? It's huge. We must have been confined to such a small area when we were kids!'

'And?' Angel was not to be dissuaded. 'If there's any ghosts they can stay well away from me. There's room for us all. Now, I think the sensible thing to do would be to put the kettle on — if we can find the kitchen — and have a cuppa. I've got the groceries in the back of the car.' Angel was nothing if not prepared and had insisted they stock up with some basics on their way to Taigh Fallon.

'I can work with that.' Zac looked down at the floorplan and then looked up again. 'That room you just appeared from. There's a corridor along there which leads to the kitchen, or the room on the other side of it — which must be the dining room — takes you in as well. I think you just found the servants' staircase.'

'Very awesome,' said Angel. She looked perfectly at home here, it had to be said. The house dated from the 1880s or thereabouts and she was dressed to complement that era — ignoring the fact she had that tattoo on the inside of her wrist. 'Now we did bring everything, didn't we? Because the alternative would be for you to go and find a shop.'

Zac pulled a face and looked around him. 'On this occasion, I'll do without anything we don't have. I can't abandon you here just yet.'

'Suits me.' Angel went over to the disguised radiator again and felt it, just as Zac had done. 'It's getting warm. That's nice. Come on.' She went back to Zac and linked his arm. 'Let's go find the kitchen. Then we'll do a little more exploring.' Her eyes were bright and the energy coming off her was phenomenal.

'I don't have a choice, do I?'

'No, you don't.' She squeezed his arm again. 'Come on. This way.'

* * *

Angel had explored the cupboards and found some mugs, and thankfully the kettle was modern and functioned well. Great Aunt Jeanie had, it seemed, not been old-fashioned enough to think that Agas and kettles set to boil on the gas flame were any better than boiling your water using electricity.

'I think I might have liked Jeanie,' said Angel, standing at the sink and staring out at the gardens. 'Do you think it would be okay to have a look at the gardens and go down to the Loch?'

'I don't see why not.' Zac set the mug down on the draining board. 'We've already used her firewood and her crockery.'

'I just think it's sweet that she left you this house.'

'She didn't just leave it to me alone,' chided Zac gently. 'It's for my whole generation, isn't it? Even the Canadian faction, if they care to surface.'

'Hopefully they won't. That kid sounds like a horrid boy. He's probably still a horrid man.' She drained her own mug and set it down next to Zac's. 'Tell me what you know about Jeanie. Come on, we'll head down to the Loch and chat about her.' She moved over to the back door and unlocked it, throwing it open to the evening air. 'Ooh petrichor.'

Angel breathed deeply. 'The smell of earth after rain. Just gorgeous.' The rain had steadied to a drizzle and it didn't seem too onerous to walk down to the Loch in it. Zac shrugged and nodded. Angel guessed that he had no objection to that, so she led the way down the winding path, where the trees met above their heads and where it traced a gentle slope to a set of stone steps which took them down to the pebbled shore of Loch Duich.

'Kyle pushed me in the Loch once. Said it was the best way to learn to swim. The water was only about a foot deep, but still. I grabbed his ankles and pulled him down with me. He wasn't happy. Anyway, as I said, the time that stands out the most from when I was little, she was dressed in black. Now I think about it, though, I wonder if it was a funeral? I'm pretty sure there was a great uncle as well, but I was just a wee bairn.' Angel smiled listening to the Scottish words roll off Zac's tongue in his lovely accent. 'So it must been, what, twenty or more years ago?' He frowned. Like Angel, he was almost twenty-nine. 'She can't have been tremendously old, though, can she?' He paused, as if trying to work it out. 'I think she was in her late nineties when she died — so yes, she could only have been in her seventies. Maybe. She was the very youngest though — I never met any of her other relatives. Just my grandfather, who was still that wee bit older than her.'

'How did she die?' asked Angel, holding onto a tree branch to steady herself as she skidded down a particularly muddy slope onto the edge of the pebbles.

'Ha!' Zac surprised her by laughing. 'You'll love this. She had been to the tea room on the high street. Had herself the biggest, creamiest wedge of cake she could find and a huge mug of hot chocolate — the whole caboodle. Whipped cream, flake, marshmallows.' He grinned out towards the arch of trees that showed a vista of the Loch opening up before him. 'She dropped dead in the street outside. Massive heart attack, they said. She never felt a thing — she'd gone before she hit the ground.'

'I can think of worse ways to go,' said Angel. 'At least she had enjoyed herself.'

'Very much so. From what my Dad said, she was never one to want to linger. She always said, 'I'll know when it's my time, and I'll go out in the way I see fit.''

'God bless her.' Angel looked up at him and smiled. 'I shouldn't be smiling, I shouldn't be happy she went, but good grief. It sounds like exactly what she would have wanted.'

Zac dropped down onto the shore beside her, abandoning the last few stone steps in favour of jumping. 'They came to the house and found everything in perfect order — she'd sent her instructions off to the solicitors a couple of weeks beforehand. Everything was in place. You can't ask for better, really. Oh!' He laughed, remembering something. 'There was bottle of whisky on the kitchen table. She'd even put a note on to say the estate agent was welcome to take it home. 'I know people think badly of you, in that job,' the note read, 'but you enjoy my little gift as a thank you. I know you'll get the best price for the youngsters.''

This time Angel did laugh, and laugh loudly. 'Bribery from beyond the grave,' she said. 'I love Jeanie, I really do. Gosh, I wish we'd met.'

'She was a character.' Zac shrugged, bent down, picked up a pebble and weighed it in his hand before skimming it across the surface of the Loch. 'But there are more of us than just me, and I'm pretty sure my cousin will appear once he's been informed. Which is why I can't get excited about Taigh Fallon. It's not properly mine. It has to be shared, but God knows how we'll do that. What if someone appears out of the woodwork, years after this place gets sold?'

'Jeanie sounds as if she made it pretty clear what she wanted,' said Angel. 'The solicitors will have it all in hand.'

'I suppose.' Zac folded his arms and stared out at the Loch. 'You get a good view of Eilean Donan here, don't you?'

'Beautiful. I spotted it before. All the bedrooms on the west look out onto it.'

Zac cast her a glance. 'You've already been in the bedrooms?'

'When I was doing my walkabout. They've all got little en suites too, which is so lovely. I've already chosen my room.'

'Why does that not surprise me?' He grinned. Good-naturedly, he pushed her. 'Oh Angel, why did it never work out between us? I know everything about you and it should have been easy.'

Angel laughed. 'I know. Maybe that's why it didn't; we know each other too well. It's the Friend Zone thing. And you're far too nice for me. I wouldn't be able to argue with you.'

'You're probably right. There's no

magic, no spark. Just Angel and Zac. A and Z with no in-betweens.'

Angel didn't take offence — it was the truth.

She nodded and picked up a handful of stones, preparing to skim them over the water; she was better at it than him and they both knew it. 'Do you think you'll ever get that spark?' she asked him. 'With anyone?'

'I hope so,' he said, watching as she took aim and sent a smooth, grey pebble bouncing across the water five times. 'Nice one.'

'Thanks.' The next one only made it four times. 'Do you think you could see yourself with someone like Ivy?' Angel looked askance at him and watched as he considered it, the idea taking shape in his brain.

'I don't know.' He pushed his hair away from his forehead, his too-long fringe flattened by the steady drizzle. 'I don't suppose she'd be interested.' He frowned.

'Why ever not? Six times! Hurrah!'

'Show off. Here, let me. Three. Not bad. I don't know — I suspect because she's got ambitions of her own and itchy feet and doesn't want to settle on a Scottish island.'

'You know this how?' Angel turned to him, wiping her hands down her skirt to get rid of the clinging mud and silt.

'It's obvious, isn't it? She's clever and she's pretty and she's talented. I told you she's wanting to go to Glastonbury. She does painting and bakes the most phenomenal cakes.' He grinned. 'Jeanie would have enjoyed them, I think. She's interested in her crystals and her holistic therapies and what use could they be where I live?'

'You said the same when you didn't know how successful the tea room would be. That's taken you by surprise — so maybe she could use her skills to help you build your business?'

'She's just renting in the town though.'

'Renting is easy enough for her to give up.'

'Maybe, but don't forget she's from the mainland.'

'So bloody what?' cried Angel. 'I despair of you. I really do.'

Zac just shook his head, then lifted his wrist and checked his watch. 'I think you're wrong, Angel, whatever ideas you may be concocting in that little gothy head of yours. But regardless, I need to get back to Skye. It's getting late and it'll take a while.' He looked up and Angel followed his gaze. The sky seemed lower than it had been; great, thick banks of cloud building up and the rain was definitely getting heavier. 'You know, I don't even know if I'm happy leaving you. It's a big old strange house.'

'And the landline is working again, and there's a decent enough mobile signal so it's not like I'll be cut off.'

'Even so. I'm not sure. You should probably come back with me. I'd be glad of the company, anyway.'

'Oh dearest Zac.' Angel flung her arms around him. 'I'm *staying*. You can collect me tomorrow. But I think you should stay too.'

'I think I should go. We should go. Last chance — you coming back?'

'Nope.' She shook her head and released him.

Zac always seemed to know when he was beaten. He smiled and dropped a quick, friendly kiss on her forehead and took her arm. 'Come on then. I'll haul you up that mud bank and make sure you're okay before I leave properly. It's no use arguing with you is it?'

'No use at all.' Angel allowed herself to be guided up the mud bank. A low rumble of thunder sounded far away and she jumped. The rain began to come down harder.

'Now is probably a good time to start running,' Zac observed.

'You're right.' Picking up her long skirt and trying to save the hem from the mud in the gardens, she lowered her head and ran as fast as she could towards Taigh Fallon.

★ ★ ★

Okay, so now it was raining. He glowered through the windows of the train at the muddy countryside. Rain. As well as being bloody cold. Kyle had no desire to half-inherit some cold, leaky house in this cold, leaky country. The sooner he had a quick look at it, decided what he wanted to do with his share, and got it off his hands, the better.

It's not like the place was in Florida or somewhere hot, was it? If he wanted cold and leaky, he'd get just as much of that at home.

6

They got back to the house before the rain got any worse. He made sure Angel was all right and had everything she needed and they hugged each other and said their goodbyes, promising to call each other later on and to see each other the next morning.

Then his 4x4 decided not to work. That, he deemed, was simply typical.

'Looks like you're staying after all.' Angel was delighted. She clapped her hands as she stood on the gravelled drive, watching him fight with the ignition. 'Seems like Jeanie has decreed it, in her own special way.'

'But I don't *want* to stay! And I don't want you to either, but it's pointless even trying to argue with you.' He popped the bonnet and climbed out of the vehicle. 'My engine might be flooded. Literally,' he said, poking around. The rain fell in big, fat drops down the back of his neck and he swore. 'I could ring the recovery service. I suppose.' Zac looked up at the darkening sky. 'But if I don't do it soon, I doubt they'll even come out in this.'

'They come anywhere, at any time, but why bother? You're right. Just leave it tonight and call them tomorrow. Do you really want to be driving all that way home in this stuff anyway?' She held her hand out, catching the raindrops, watching as they bounced out of her palm and made a waterfall through her fingers. 'Live a little, Zachary. Please.'

Zac slammed the bonnet down and scowled at the sky. 'It certainly does seem as if this is in for the night.'

'Then that's a good enough reason for you to hole up here with me. Look at it — two hundred miles! You wouldn't get two hundred yards. Good car.' She patted the scratched, navy blue bonnet.

'Good car?' Zac snorted in disgust.

'Pile of junk, more like it. I guess I'm with you for the evening then.' He frowned. 'And I guess I need to call Ivy to let her know. She'll need to close up and goodness knows where that leaves me for tomorrow.'

'Surely she can open up as well?' The issue was clearly *not* an issue with Angel. 'I'm positive she's competent enough to do that.'

'She might feel it's an imposition, or that I've done it deliberately.'

'She'll think nothing of the sort. Just call her, explain about the car and she'll be fine.' A shrug. Nothing was a bother.

'Hmmm,' muttered Zac. 'I'm still going to apologise to her.' The rain was relentlessly falling, dripping off the leaves, and creating puddles beneath the trees. 'I'll just tell her it's real Scottish rain and she'll understand,' he said, ironically.

He didn't really mind spending the evening with Angel — but part of him had definitely been looking forward to returning to his croft.

'So,' Angel said, throwing the comment over her shoulder as she practically danced back to the house, 'which bedroom do you want? You can have any of them, so long as I get the first one on the left of the staircase.'

7

Angel opened her carpet bag and took out her overnight clothes. She looked at the big, wooden wardrobe and decided she might as well go the whole way and hang her clothes up in it, instead of keeping them in the bag or decorating the other furniture with them as she usually did.

She could pretend she lived here for a start; take on a different persona, one from say 1897, one that fitted with the way she looked and the way she sometimes felt when faced with the modern-day world. One that matched the way she felt when cobbled old Church Street in Whitby sometimes seemed to blur and shift, and slip back a couple of hundred years.

She was certain that she wasn't the only person who wanted to retreat into the past, just for a little while. Just to recharge her batteries. She wouldn't want to stay there permanently — she enjoyed her life too much. But sometimes, it was tempting.

She shook her clothes out — short taffeta dress, long black velvet skirt, corseted top with a sweetheart neckline, a red, voluminous net petticoat (which folded up very small, probably because it was mainly layers of net with air between them) and a couple of other items — and opened the wardrobe door.

That old-wardrobe smell assailed her nostrils — something like leather and moth balls and varnished wood and dust — and she pulled out some hangers. It didn't take long to put her clothes in there and she touched the sea of inkiness, pleased.

She pulled back the candlewick bedcover and ran her hand across the mattress, smoothing some creases out. The housekeeping agency had done a good job yesterday; the bedding smelled fresh and clean, the room was perfectly neat and aired, not having that aura of neglect that might have been expected.

She had procured the room she wanted. Zac was two rooms along and had moaned rather consistently since he realised he was trapped here for the evening. But currently, his door was shut, they had found some of Jeanie's whisky, wrestled with their consciences very briefly, then raised a glass to her. Afterwards, they'd kissed each other on the cheeks and retired to their respective rooms. Zac would, no doubt, be fast asleep by now; he could sleep on a clothesline.

Once she was satisfied with the bed, Angel turned to the door. Beyond that, a couple of steps along the corridor, was the short staircase to the attics. The light in the room flickered, the storm outside raging, battering against the old stonework. It was coming in from the west relentlessly. She padded over to the window and flung it wide, leaning out so the rain soaked her skin and the wind whipped her hair around, straining her eyes to see the shadow of Eilean Donan on the opposite shores. She thought she saw it, a darker shadow than its backdrop, but she might have been mistaken. She inhaled deeply, her soul expanding with sheer exhilaration of being here, on the west coast of Scotland, right in the middle of a storm. The air hung heavy with the promise of thunder and lightning and Angel smiled into the darkness.

She withdrew, back into the room and shut the window. Much as she loved the fresh air, she had a feeling the rain, falling horizontally, as it seemed, would soak her bed through in two minutes flat. Best to shut the weather out and explore that attic before daylight claimed Taigh Fallon again. The attic would not be quite so atmospheric in the daylight, she thought. So she headed to the door and pulled it open, stepping into the panelled corridor and walking towards the staircase that so intrigued her.

1897

'Follow me.' Annis was decisive, walking ahead of Alasdair, holding her

skirts up as she made her way through the entrance hall up the wide, oak staircase.

'Let me reset the fire for you,' he said, trying to stave off her progress. 'It's chilly and if the servants have gone for the evening . . .'

'I care nought for heat or fires, Alasdair. I care only for what I must do.'

He followed her up the stairs, the gas lamps flickering, casting shadows in the nooks and crannies of the hallway.

'Please, Annis.' Alasdair reached out, touching her shoulder.

'No!' She swung around, the taffeta rustling against the floorboards. 'If you ever love someone as much as I loved him, you would want to do this as well. All you have to do is come with me. You're the only person I can trust. Look.' She turned and pointed to the small staircase up into the attics. 'It's just up here. Everything is ready.'

'But I don't see what you can — '

'Hush!' she said angrily. 'You will see. I pray that you will see.'

8

Angel poised at the bottom of the small staircase and looked up, delicious shivers running up her spine as some shadows melted away from the steps and seemed to vanish upwards. Whatever moonlight was struggling through the rainclouds must be reaching along here as well and playing tricks on her eyes. There was a closed door at the top of the staircase, and she hoped against hope it wasn't locked. She looked behind her, along the corridor towards Zac's room. She didn't really want to go knocking on his door this close to midnight, asking for sets of keys he may or may not know the location of.

She turned back to the staircase and stepped, determinedly, onto it. Her heart began beating a little faster and she took another step towards the door. Four more steps, and she was there.

She reached out and turned the handle, hearing the little *click* as it opened.

'Thank you!' Angel murmured, to no one in particular, and stepped into the cold, dark corridor beyond. She hesitated then turned left along the corridor. That way, she thought, might lead to the wonderful little tower at the edge of the house. A cold breeze whispered past her as she walked along the corridor. She held her skirt up, the fabric rustling as she made her way to the tower room.

★　★　★

The corridor ended at an arched doorway, blocked by a heavy wooden door which stood ajar. A shaft of flickering light broke through the crack, as if candles lit the room from the other side.

Angel's heart leapt, quashing down the notion that someone was in there already, remembering briefly that fleeting darkness on the staircase. She paused, wary of opening the door. It seemed to her as if voices were whispering, their words unclear but defined, somehow, in the midnight world beyond.

But how ridiculous. There was only her and Zac here, and he was in his bedroom on the floor below her.

Unless — she perked up — perhaps his room led to the tower room and he was the one in there. Of course. Angel smiled and threw open the door, ready to greet Zac with a loud '*Surprise!*'

The whispering stopped and the room suddenly held nothing but the shadows of the trees outside, branches waving and brushing against the window panes, criss-crossing the room in spikes of moon-light.

Angel let her skirts drop and walked in, looking around her. All there was in the room was a round, dark wood table with a thin layer of dust on it, two very upright chairs upholstered in faded red velvet and a spindly-legged table with an ornate, oval mirror on it. Sconces were on the walls, filled with the stumps of long-burned-out candles and two more candlesticks were positioned either side of the mirror.

The room had three large leaded windows which looked out south, east and west; the western aspect framing the ruins of Eilean Donan castle across the Loch. At the moment, there were rolling clouds filling the night sky; a smudged fingerprint of a full moon silvering the landscape when it managed to break through.

And it was cold, bloody cold, even if it *was* just April. A draught gusted down through the chimney and Angel shivered, folding her arms about her and walking over to the western window. The castle was looming over the distant shores and she leaned on the windowsill, watching the place as if it would suddenly change in some way; make itself whole again, perhaps the shades of the long dead Mackenzies and Macraes spilling out onto the bridge that led up to the place.

A sigh arrested her attention. No — a sob. It sounded like a woman, choking back some sort of emotion, just behind her, and she spun around. The moon vanished completely behind a cloud and plunged the room into velvety darkness. Angel stumbled, tripping on the hem of her dress and lurched forward, grabbing the corner of the spindly-legged table. The mirror shifted its angle as the table tilted and Angel found herself staring at her reflection, her face even paler than usual, wide-eyed and ethereal.

Beyond her reflection, was another shadow. It resolved itself into the shape of a man, his face as pale as Angel's, the planes of his cheekbones sharply defined. His eyes were black, his hair even blacker.

Angel squeaked out a strange little noise, and reached out to the glass, the moonlight catching on her jet ring. The man reflected there shifted his gaze and for a moment their eyes met. He raised his hand, and the first flash of lightning lit up the sky outside the tower. Angel jumped and transferred her attention to the window. A tree branch smashed against the window, followed by a barrage of rain.

When she looked back at the mirror, all she saw reflected was herself and the back-to-front image of the empty tower room.

Angel didn't stay long enough to see if that changed; instead, she hitched up her skirt and scurried out of the room. She made sure the door to the tower room was pulled firmly shut and ran along the corridor, back to the staircase that led down to the bedrooms.

By the time she had reached her own room and shut the door behind her, flooding her room with light as she snapped the switch on, her heart rate had returned to normal and she had begun to doubt what she had seen.

It was, surely, just an old room in an old-lady house that had probably been a very pleasant reading room or sewing room for a previous old-lady resident.

Nothing to worry about. Nothing at all.

She was still telling herself that as she shed her clothing and slipped into a red, satin nightgown. By the time she had slipped beneath the cool cotton sheets and pulled the pink candlewick bedspread up, she believed it. A place such as Taigh Fallon was bound to play tricks on a person's imagination, wasn't it? She decided *not* to tell Zac that one. She could imagine what he would say to her. No — she had a vivid imagination, and she'd let the atmosphere get to her.

Men who weren't there just didn't reflect in mirrors. It simply didn't happen.

1897

There had been, he swore, a woman in the looking glass. She had stared at him as he had stared at her. Her hair was dark and long and loose. It framed her pale, serious face and something like a diamond had glinted at the side of her nose. There were strange markings on her inner wrist and for a split second their eyes had met and he felt a jolt of electricity, a shiver throughout his body.

Annis sat at the table behind him, muttering charms and incantations.

He did not listen to her. Instead, he stared at the mirror, willing the woman to return to him — and whether she was angel or demon, he found he did not care.

9

Angel lay in the wide bed, the curtains open to the storm. It was now pitch black outside, but somehow the branches were even darker, waving and bending under the force of the wind. Rain battered the windows and far over Loch Duich, jagged lightning lit up the ruins of Eilean Donan castle.

Strange men in the mirror aside, it was, actually, quite delicious.

Angel wiggled her toes under the heavy bedspread and fitted her hands beneath her head, staring into the darkness. She let her mind drift and tried to imagine what it had been like so many years ago. Taigh Fallon was the sort of place she had only dreamed about. She wished with all her heart that she had a couple of million pounds — enough to buy this house and still keep on her dear little Goth Cottage at

Whitby. She'd travel up and down Britain, coming here every couple of weeks — by private jet, why not, if she was a millionaire — and have enough money to employ an assistant in her workshop. Then she could leave her business unattended, quite happily and on a much more frequent basis.

She shifted in bed, sighing and turning on her side to get a better view of the storm. She could dream. Nobody had ever come to grief by dreaming.

She wondered, again, if she'd been dreaming earlier, when she had seen that image in the mirror. She tried to picture the man once more, squeezing her eyes shut and attempting to drag his image to the forefront of her mind. It had just been a fleeting glimpse, if that. And it had been quite late and the room had been quite spooky. She suspected it must have been a figment of her imagination, but —

She stiffened, her heart pounding.

People had, however, come to grief by people breaking into their houses in the middle of the night. And if she wasn't mistaken, that noise from downstairs was the door crashing open and shutting again.

10

He came in, shaking the worst of the storm from his clothing, brushing the raindrops angrily from his shoulders. Leaky and cold. As he suspected. And that was just the weather.

He paused in the entrance hall, dropping his bag on the floor just as he spotted the dying fire and the heat-bright embers in the grate. He quickly stuffed the papers in his pocket, his heart beginning to thump against his chest.

He stopped, looking sharply across at the sweeping oak staircase. There was a noise, a footfall at the top. A breath — a creak as the footfall shifted. His heart pounding, he moved over to the fireplace, his gaze never leaving the staircase. He took hold of the poker, grasping it firmly as he crossed the room.

He raised the poker, and walked

slowly up to the first, small landing.

'*Who the hell are you?*'

He was not prepared for that — not prepared for a strong, female voice with an English accent challenging him.

Torchlight flashed across him, making him wince and turn his face away from it. However, he stood his ground.

'Who the hell are *you?*' he shouted back, equally strongly. He glared into the beam of light. 'I own this place. And I'm calling the police.'

★   ★   ★

There was a beat.

'Zac!' screeched Angel, turning tail and scurrying up the staircase, back along the corridor. 'Zac! There's a man in the house. Call the police. He's armed.'

She grasped hold of Zac's door handle and flung herself into his room. 'Quickly! Barricade the door!' She shot the bolt and began dragging a chair across the door, as Zac sat straight up in bed, swearing.

85

'He's coming,' Angel continued. 'Oh God! He's going to kill us!' She began to sob and turned her attention to the dressing table. 'Help me, Zac! Don't just lie there! Bloody hell!'

'What are you saying?' cried Zac, fully awake now. 'A man? Where?'

'Here! In the house. Listen!' She gestured to the door as running footsteps pounded along the hallway. There was a rap at the door, a rattle of the door handle.

A loud, accented masculine voice shouted outside: 'Come out! Before I break this door down! This is my house, you're trespassing.' He hammered on the door, seemingly with the poker and Angel flew to the other side of the bed. She reasoned if it came to it, she would do her utmost to jump out of the window and run away.

'Who the hell are you?' shouted Zac. 'This is *my* house.' He scrambled out of bed and flicked the light switch on, grabbing his mobile phone from the bedside table.

'None of your business!' shouted the man, 'and I don't give a damn who you are.'

Zac bristled. 'I'm Zac Fallon,' he answered, equally loudly. 'And I've every right to be here. This was my great aunt's house and it's mine now. You've got ten seconds to leave or I call the police.'

The hammering on the door stopped, and Angel imagined the man pausing, his poker halfway to the door.

'Zac Fallon?' The voice was steadier, although still simmering with anger.

'Yes.' Zac looked at Angel and shrugged his shoulders. 'Five seconds.'

There was the sound of something which might have been a half-hearted attempt at a short, unamused laugh.

'Long time, no see, Cousin Zac. It's Kyle. Kyle Fallon. This is my house as well. Left to me by Great Aunt Jeanie.'

'The Canadian faction,' snapped Angel. 'It's the *cousin*!' She stared at Zac, her eyes wide. 'The mean one. The one that broke your Action Man and hid the books — God, if Jessie ever found that out — that he made books inaccessible to a *child*! What shall we do? I hate him already!' She could place that accent now she knew he was Canadian. Working where she did, she experienced quite a variety of accents. But then, answering her own question, she found herself shouting at the door: 'Prove it! Prove you're a Fallon.'

'Are *you* a Fallon as well?' came the response, brusque and annoyed.

'No. I'm a Tempest.' Angel found that she was no longer scared, just very angry that this mean-spirited cousin should turn up and appear inside the house. 'But before you go staking a claim to Zac's inheritance I want some proof you're who you say you are.'

'Angel!' Zac glared at her. 'Shut up.'

'No!' hissed Angel. 'He could be anybody.'

'For God's sake!' shouted the man. 'Here. Look here, dammit.' Some papers came under the door, shoved rather angrily through the gap, spinning and skidding to a halt before Angel's feet. She bent down and retrieved them, scanning through them silently before she handed them over to Zac. They seemed to be identical to the ones that Zac had shown her about the house. At the bottom of the last page were the words *Enc: One Key*. Exactly as they had been on Zac's letter. He was telling the truth then. He had every right to be here — more than she did, really. There was also a credit card with his name emblazoned on the front, which had skittered along the floorboards and was staring mockingly at her. He was clearly too smart to post his passport through the gap; credit cards could be cancelled if they refused to return the documents.

'Now I want to see some proof *you're* a Fallon,' snarled this Kyle person.

Angel's hackles rose once more. How *dare* he be rude to Zac! She made her mind up there and then to dislike the man. Any enemy of Zac's was an enemy of hers.

'Sure,' replied Zac, sighing. He got to his feet and rummaged through his wallet. 'Here. Here's my driving licence. I've got the same paperwork as you, if you want to see it.'

There was a pause. 'No. I trust you.' A muffled half-laugh again. 'Not like your friend in there. Shall we deal with this like adults, Zac?'

The driving licence came back through the gap and Angel pounced on it, before handing it back to Zac.

'Aye. It sounds like the best plan to me,' replied Zac with a sigh. He pulled on his T-shirt and jeans, apparently not caring that the whole scenario that had just gone before had been played out with him in his boxer shorts and Angel in a floaty, red satin nightgown topped by a black satin robe. Angel could understand that. They'd known each other too long to be bothered with that sort of stuff.

'We'll have to chat it through,' he said to her. 'He's probably as confused as we are.'

Angel pulled a face behind his back as she followed him to the door. She quickly rearranged her features before he scraped the chair away from the door, moved the dressing table a little to get around it — she hadn't dragged it very far, really — and undid the bolt.

Peering over Zac's shoulder, Angel stopped short. The world shifted as there before her stood the man who she had seen in the mirror, albeit briefly. Who could forget those eyes and those sharp planes of his cheekbones?

Not her. That was for sure.

She wondered whether he had found another entrance to that tower room, whether he had been hiding in there all along and had run when she spotted his reflection. Taigh Fallon might indeed be a house full of secret passages, and that had given that awful man an advantage.

She really did hate him already.

11

Kyle stared back at the girl who was looking at him as if she'd seen a ghost. She was the one who had, crazily, challenged him on the stairs. He was the innocent party.

She pulled a robe of some description closer together, covering a red satin nightgown and Kyle caught sight of a tattoo on her inside wrist. Light glinted off a diamond stud in her nose and her hair was jet black, hanging straight down from a centre parting, curling in little ringlets at the ends, way down past her shoulders. Her face was pale in the fitful moonlight streaming through the stained glass windows at the end of the hallway, her eyes dark, her chin pointed and thrust out haughtily or defensively — he couldn't quite work it out. Kyle had recently seen a waxwork of Anne Boleyn, Henry VIII's unfortunate second wife — this girl could easily have modelled for that.

'Is there a light switch somewhere?' he asked, turning his attention to the man standing next to her: his cousin Zac, who he hadn't seen for twenty years or so. And this woman's partner, by all appearances, although chalk and cheese might have been a good way to describe the unlikely coupling. Zac had too-long, mousey-coloured hair, almost blonde in the light. He appeared to be a dreamer; a vague, half-asleep look in his eyes, an aura of calm and peace around him. He seemed out of place here, in the midst of a thunderstorm. Perhaps that was why he was blinking like a bemused dormouse, dragged out of its nest.

The woman, on the other hand, would not be out of place haunting a cemetery.

'I think there's a switch just along here,' said his cousin. 'Excuse me.' He sidled past, Kyle stepping back to let him grope his way along the wall. 'Ah.

Here we are.' There was a little click as the light came on and flooded the corridor. The girl — Anne Boleyn — squinted and dipped her head, retreating into the shadows.

Kyle stared at her, fascinated, half-wondering if she was indeed a vampire.

But there was something more. He knew her, he was sure. He'd seen her somewhere before; but as the demons she quite clearly controlled mocked his farthest-flung memories he was at a loss. There was just a look in her eyes that told him more than he actually felt comfortable knowing at this precise moment in time.

He shuddered. He didn't think he wanted to take that thought much further.

'Shall we take this downstairs?' his cousin was saying. 'Might be better than up here.' Zac was studying Kyle as curiously as Kyle had studied him, no doubt wondering what a rain-soaked guy of over six foot was doing with a poker in his hand. He must have been at least a foot shorter last time they met. Kyle hadn't shaved for a couple of days and he knew his chin would be dusted with dark stubble. Likewise, his almost-black hair was curling around the edges with the dampness. And he knew he would be scowling. He always scowled when he was out of temper, and tonight he was very much out of temper.

'Downstairs would be good,' he said. He glanced at Anne Boleyn, and was darkly amused to see she possessed a scowl to match his own. He half-smiled. She was braver now the light was on and her boyfriend was between them. 'I must say, though, that you, Miss, don't seem to be a member of the family.' He couldn't help it, even though it was pretty childish. 'I guess my question would be what are *you* doing here? In our great aunt's home?'

The girl pulled herself straight, flashing him a truly demonic look.

She opened her mouth to either curse him or respond, but Zac put his hand on her arm and answered instead. 'Angel's with me. Now, let's go downstairs.' He gestured with his arm, a sweeping, courtly, old-fashioned gesture indicating that they should turn tail and head back to the entrance hall. If she was Anne Boleyn, he was one of those poor guys she'd taken down with her.

But she was called Angel. How ironic.

★　★　★

'Arrogant sod,' muttered Angel in Zac's ear as they followed Kyle down the stairs. 'And look. He's dripping on the staircase. He might have taken his boots off.'

'Probably the last thing on his mind,' murmured Zac. He paused to press another switch, bathing the entrance hall in light this time.

Kyle, meanwhile, had dripped his way downstairs and now stood in the hall, looking up at them, still glowering, still holding that damn poker.

'You can put the poker away,' said Angel. 'We're not dangerous.'

Kyle looked at her for a moment. 'Maybe he's not,' he said, gesturing to Zac with the implement, 'but I can't speak for you.'

Angel called him something unsavoury under her breath and swept past him to the sofa in front of the very nearly dead fire. 'You think yourself lucky I didn't shove you down the stairs,' she said.

'You think yourself lucky I didn't go for you with this,' he snapped, brandishing it again.

'Okay, okay,' said Zac. 'Here, give that to me before someone gets hurt.' He held his hand out for the poker and Kyle relinquished it grudgingly. 'Now,' said Zac, putting it back beside the fire, 'let's get this straight. You inherited this place from our great aunt Jeanie. So did I.'

Kyle nodded. 'Yes. That codicil said it was to be left to the younger generation.' He frowned, his dark brows lowering and meeting, giving him a particularly demonic look. 'I kind of knew I wouldn't be the only one. But hey — ' He spread his hands out then folded his arms tightly across his front, ' — I didn't expect anyone else to be here tonight. Certainly not that little guy I used to torment.' He grinned and Angel bristled again. *Torment!* God, how mean he must have been!

Kyle Fallon continued, oblivious, it seemed, to the fact he was simply not endearing himself to Angel Tempest. 'I flew in from Ontario on the world's longest damn flight yesterday, and picked up a train on the country's slowest damn railway today. Because I decided to come here.'

'But when do you go *back*?' Angel bit out the comment, knowing she sounded dangerously polite. And she wasn't being polite. Not at all. And she hoped this man would understand that.

Kyle turned to face her. 'I have an open-ended ticket, Morticia. It's entirely up to me, arrogant sod that I am. I also have excellent hearing.'

Angel felt the colour flood her cheeks. She folded her arms and turned pointedly away from him, staring into the fire. As if on cue, thunder rumbled overhead and lightning lit up the room through the stained glass.

'Okay,' said Zac again, ever the peacemaker. Just in the corner of her vision, Angel saw him make a calm down sort of gesture, patting the air in front of him. 'Well, I got the same information as you. And the same key, it seems. I live on the Isle of Skye now, and just meant to come here for a visit. The weather turned though, and my car broke and I got stranded.'

'*She* looks as if she was prepared to stay,' growled Kyle. Angel knew he would be nodding towards her and her satin nightgown

She turned and glared at him. '*She* didn't expect to encounter a creep on the staircase though.'

'For God's sake!' yelped Zac. Angel stared at him. It was quite possibly one of the only times she had heard him almost lose his temper. 'Yes, she brought an overnight bag. That's my fault. I said she could stay here on her own if she wanted to. Angel is not the sort of person you throw a challenge like that down to and expect her to refuse.'

Kyle glanced at her, glowering, and returned his attention to Zac. 'Fair enough. You couldn't have predicted I was coming here.'

Angel raised her eyebrows. She felt like dancing around singing 'Hallelujah'. The man had capitulated. 'Hallelujah' indeed. Instead, she sat down, huffily, on the long bench by the fireplace.

'I knew you were out there,' said Zac with a little smile. He sat down next to Angel. 'But that's all I knew. I didn't think you'd turn up here tonight, you're right.'

'Well I'm glad you had the forethought to get the electricity working,' replied Kyle. 'It was something I never thought of. I guess I just expected to bed down for the night, have a look around in the morning and decide what to do with my share of it. As it is, we

100

appear to have fifty percent of a house each.' His face contorted in what on anybody else might have been a smile.

Zac presumably took it as such and smiled back. 'Fifty percent. I guess we need to speak to the solicitors just to make sure nobody else is going to come knocking.' He held his hand out to Kyle, who hesitated just a second then took it. The two men shook hands, seemingly happy to go halves on the place and sort the finer details out the following day.

Angel's heart was by now somewhere near her toes. She didn't know what *she* had expected from Taigh Fallon, let alone what Zac had expected; but to have to share the place tonight — any night — with an unpleasant Canadian had not been on her agenda. She might have been a little more accommodating had he not been so — arrogant. And scary. Yes. *Scary* on those stairs. And she couldn't forgive him for being vile to Little Zac.

Angel was pretty good at holding

grudges — either her own or on someone else's behalf. This wasn't going to go away easily.

Kyle nodded, then yawned. 'Sounds good to me,' he said. 'Sorry. I suppose I'd better get going before I do crash here. I think there's a hotel down the road. I'll see if they've got any rooms.' Kyle pulled a mobile phone from his pocket, presumably to search for details of the hotel.

'Don't be daft,' said Zac standing up again. 'This place is as much yours as it is mine. I'm not going to stop you from staying. There are plenty of rooms. Besides, I wouldn't turn a dog out into that weather, never mind a relative.'

'Zac!' Angel shot to her feet. 'But he was *mean* to you!'

'And we were kids and it's tipping it down out there. Come on, Kyle. Let's point you in the right direction for the bathroom. You can get dried out and choose a bedroom.' Zac must have sensed Angel bristling. Their rooms were on the western side of the house, so they could see the ruins of Eilean Donan. Well, so *she* could see the ruins of Eilean Donan. Zac hadn't really cared.

'We're on the left side of the house. You might want to use one of the rooms on the right.'

Kyle flicked a glance at Angel, his dark eyes flashing. 'I will *definitely* take the right.' He leaned down and shouldered his travel bag.

Angel stood up, making it plain her intention was to retire to bed. 'Come on Zac. Let's go to bed.' She grabbed him by the arm and linked him. Head held high, she stalked towards the staircase dragging her friend in her wake.

There was a muffled snort of what may have been derisive laughter from Kyle, but she ignored him and instead continued up the staircase. As they passed the window on the half-landing, another barrage of rain battered the glass and another flash of lightning lit up the staircase. She heard Kyle's footsteps behind her but did not look back.

Once they were inside Zac's room, she shut the door soundly and listened at the crack to ensure Kyle had turned away to the right.

Satisfied the footsteps were heading away from the room, she exhaled a breath she wasn't aware she was holding. 'Thank the Lord for that,' she said.

'Angel!'

But she shushed Zac with a hiss and a flap of her hand until she was entirely satisfied she had heard a door shut somewhere along the corridor.

'He's gone.' She flung herself dramatically against the door and tipped her head backwards, resting it there and closing her eyes. 'Honestly!' She lifted her head and fixed Zac with a look. 'Unbelievable.'

'Angel, are you going back to your room?' He sounded tired, climbing into bed after discarding his T-shirt and jeans in a crumpled heap on the floor.

'The Hell I am.' She discarded her satin robe next to his pile of clothes and climbed into bed next to him. 'You think I'm going to my bedroom alone with a strange man in the house? Think again.'

'He's not a strange man,' said Zac sleepily. He turned over, his back to Angel as she lay on her back. 'He's my cousin and it's late and he'll be trauchled.'

Trauchled. A Scottish word for exhausted. Hmmm. Angel flipped onto her side, her back to his, and stared out into the room. She'd lost her view of the castle, because Zac had taken that side of the bed. She sighed. But the only response she got was Zac's slow, steady breathing as he fell into what seemed to be a deep, delicious sleep.

Sometimes, she hated Zac.

1897

He looked into the mirror, the room reflected oddly behind him. Annis was in the background, drifting around and blowing the candles out one by one.

'I didn't see him,' she said, close to tears. 'He didn't come back to me.'

'He's at peace, Annis,' he said, distracted. He reached his fingertips to the glass. It was smooth and cold beneath his touch. 'Perhaps he won't come, if he's at peace.'

She swung around, steadying herself on the table. Her eyes were red-rimmed, her other hand supporting her swollen abdomen. 'But I'm not at peace! How can he be at peace?'

He had no answer for her. 'Isn't this just a nonsense?' he asked. 'A séance. Trying to talk to the dead.' He turned to face her. 'I miss him too. He was my brother!'

'But he was my husband!' she cried. She collapsed into a chair and resting on the table, laid her head on her arms.

He sat down opposite her, moving the letters and numbers aside. They made him uncomfortable. He didn't think it was right.

'Annis, you could be calling anything back. We don't know enough about this. I know you've read about it, but — '

'Why won't he come back to me,' she cried, her voice muffled. 'Why won't he come back?'

Alasdair laid his hand on her head, smoothing her hair back. He felt sorry for her, he truly did; but that woman he'd seen. The one with the dark hair and the dark eyes and the pale, pale face. His gaze drifted back to the mirror. He saw again the strange markings on her body, the roses and the vines on her wrist. The glint of a diamond at the side of her nose. She was nothing like he had seen before. But he had, for a single moment, felt that she was looking back at him, as curious and as intrigued as he was.

He looked back at Annis, her shoulders heaving as she sobbed into her arms. He couldn't share that vision with her; he didn't even know if it was real. It appeared as if Annis, his beautiful mistake, had summoned something or someone up; he just didn't know who the woman was or where on earth — or beyond — she had come from.

12

Kyle stomped towards the rooms on the right hand side of the staircase, cursing Anne Boleyn or Morticia or whatever he wanted to call her. He didn't want to call her Angel. She wasn't one, not at all. Demon. He could call her Demon. Demona. That suited her.

He flung the door open to the first room he came to, groped around for a light switch then dropped his bag on the bed. The taxi had left him at the entrance gates and he'd walked up the gravelled driveway towards the looming, black house at the end. He had known that it would be beautiful in the daytime, but tonight it had looked like something from a horror movie with the storm breaking above it, moving across from that ruined castle. It was no wonder he'd thought the place had been broken into when he'd seen the fireplace.

His cousin seemed okay — sensible, a guy he could get on with it. He felt a little guilty about the way he had treated him when they were kids, but Zac seemed cool about it, which was a blessing. He could have made things very difficult tonight, if he'd been so inclined.

That woman though — she was anything but okay. If the place had been a horror movie set, she would have been a vampire, sweeping down the staircase hunting for blood.

He pitied his poor cousin. How the hell had he got himself enmeshed with that creature?

He flung the wardrobe open and threw some clothes hangers onto the bed, then pulled his sodden clothing off. He realised that his clothes probably wouldn't dry in the wardrobe, so he shoved them roughly onto the hangers and hooked them over another door which led into a little ensuite bathroom. They might drip dry, if he was lucky.

At least, he thought, *I don't have to bump into her when I'm looking for a shower in the morning.*

He cleaned his teeth and washed his face, running his hand over his chin, deciding whether it was worth shaving or not. Hell no. He might tomorrow morning. But not now. Then he headed back across the room, snapped the light off and slipped in between the sheets.

With one, heavy turn, he closed his eyes and almost immediately fell asleep. He knew that he was still scowling at the memory of that dark-haired woman with her flashing eyes and her huge attitude problem.

★ ★ ★

The dream came slowly to him at first, creeping insidiously around the darkest edges of his consciousness. She was in it — Anne, or Morticia or Demona. He still didn't know what to call her. But she was there.

She was on the other side of a mirror.

111

He was standing in a circular room, staring into an oval glass, and in it he saw three images: he saw himself, unshaven and dark-eyed, his cheeks shadowed and hollowed out — the result of too much whisky and too little sleep.

There was a woman behind him, moving slowly and painfully, snuffing out candles one by one, quietly sobbing. She was garbed in a voluminous black dress, unflattering to her complexion, which was the typical pale-faced, freckled, skin of the true redhead. Looking back at him, through that mirror, was Angel.

He could call her Angel here — for that was what she was, was it not? The Angel of Death. Was she to come for him as she had come for Connor? Or had she come for Annis or perhaps the child within her? Connor's child; she swore it was Connor's child, although he, Alasdair, knew better. So did she. It was guilt that drove her to do this and Alasdair, bearer of his own guilt, had *encouraged her.*

Annis. Connor. Alasdair. How did he know their names?

'Angel,' he murmured, reaching his fingertips out to her. They touched cold glass and she was still there, behind it, watching him. He would welcome her when she finally came.

This was not the first time he had seen her, not at all. He had seen her before. God forgive him, but he had no interest in speaking to Connor. Connor, who had everything to live for, until he found out, and then that was an end to it all.

Alasdair was only interested in his Angel, the Angel with the strange markings on her skin and the dark eyes that matched his own.

The babe, when it came, would have those eyes as well. Luckily, he and his brother shared those eyes, which would make it all so much easier . . .

Kyle awoke with a start as a crash of thunder broke directly overhead and the room split in two with lightning. He hadn't shut the curtains, thinking that nothing would rouse him. He hadn't bargained on that dream. He hadn't bargained on any dream affecting him to that extent. He stared into the darkness, waiting for his heart rate to calm down and remembering discordant parts of the dream.

Frustrated, he turned over. She had no right to invade his dreams — no right at all.

It was only a few seconds later that his eyes snapped open and his heart hammered in his chest. It wasn't the first time she'd invaded his dreams. That was where he knew her from before.

★   ★   ★

Angel dozed off, rigid and seething in the bed next to Zac, hating dark, brooding Canadians with a vengeance. She didn't doze for very long though. She was wide awake at three o'clock, sighing into the darkness. Her dreams had been weird and spooky, and involved too much of someone who looked too much like Kyle Fallon and had dark, stormy eyes that she was drowning in — quite willingly, it seemed . . .

Which was hideous. Absolutely hideous.

And besides, that, there was something about that room upstairs; something she couldn't put her finger on. All she knew, was that she didn't like the idea that Kyle had potentially discovered a secret entrance to it and hadn't just appeared downstairs, all innocent like he claimed.

Throwing the covers off, Angel slid out of bed and padded over to the doorway. She was going back into that tower.

She hurried up the little staircase and along the corridor, throwing the door open. Standing in the middle of the room, she looked around, hearing nothing but the sound of her pulse in her ears. She caught sight of the mirror and strode across to it, standing squarely in front of it and peering into the glass.

He was there again, drifting into her

line of vision. Angel gasped and spun around, seeing if he was behind her, creeping around the room, scowling, as was his wont.

But she was alone. The voices that she had heard earlier in the evening were gathering pace, whispering around her like a rushing whirlwind. She cast one last glance into the mirror and saw him reach out for her again; then she turned tail and fled back to Zac and the comforting safety of his oblivious snores.

13

Angel sat at the breakfast table the next day, twisting the mourning ring round and round her finger, thinking about the tower room.

She looked up sharply as the door opened and Kyle stormed in, his brow furrowed, scowling at the world. He noticed her and stopped short, looking as if he wanted to say something.

'Good morning, Kyle,' said Angel. No way was he going to ignore her. 'Help yourself to tea or coffee. You're welcome, by the way.' She waved across at the bench.

'No thanks. You might have poisoned it.'

'I have better things to waste my time on than poisoning strangers. Even if they do creep around at night and have a history of terrorising smaller children. You might as well have something.

117

Coffee might cheer you up.'

'I'm not used to making conversation over breakfast. So you'll excuse me, I'm sure, if I just ignore you.'

Angel shrugged. 'Please yourself.'

'I will, thanks.'

The sarcastic tone of voice did not endear him to her and Angel wondered whether he would condescend to sit with her. It was a large, scrubbed wooden table and there was plenty of room on it — but wherever he sat, she had a feeling it would be too close.

They were spared that horror by a very dishevelled Zac stumbling in, rubbing his eyes and yawning.

His gaze, once he had focused on them, took in the kettle and the unopened milk. He headed towards the stuff like an arrow.

'Did you sleep okay?' Zac threw the comment out to anyone who was listening. 'And does anyone want a cuppa? I'm making myself one.'

'Yeah. A coffee would be great,' replied Kyle. Angel felt herself flush with anger. *After he'd refused one she had offered!* 'And I guess I slept okay.' The man was evasive about that one, and Angel looked at him as he moved across to Zac and accepted a mug from him.

Kyle studied his coffee rather more than Angel thought necessary and leaned against the bench. He clearly wasn't sitting down. Angel wondered if he had been wandering about finding secret entrances to tower rooms instead of sleeping.

'I had some weird dreams, but you know.' Kyle flicked a glance at Angel, his face unreadable. She turned her attention back to her ring — it was jet, of course, and set with a flower picked out in diamonds on the broad, black oval face. She was glad she'd worn it — it showed some respect for poor Jeanie, whose kitchen they were all sitting in and whose whisky, God bless her, they'd broken into. Angel had a feeling Jeanie would have encouraged the youngsters to enjoy themselves in her house though, and she allowed herself a small smile.

'Aye,' acknowledged Zac. 'It can get to you.'

What 'it' was, Angel was not entirely certain, but she refused to believe anything could get to this chap enough to stop him sleeping. He seemed too distant from reality, too wrapped up in himself to care.

She chose to ignore the dreams she vaguely remembered from last night, but annoyingly the thought of those eyes in her dream made her blush and she couldn't bring herself to look at the man who seemed to possess those eyes in real life.

Zac, happily oblivious as always, headed to the bench and popped two slices of bread into the toaster. 'Chocolate spread for our breakfast,' he commented, seeing the open pot next to the toaster. He turned to Angel. 'You?'

She nodded. 'It was easier.'

'Good choice.'

'It was, but it hardly matters now. I thought I could have gone shopping if I needed to, but I'll be packing my things back up today, so it's a moot point.'

Zac nodded. 'I suppose, under the circumstances, we'll have to go back today anyway — if I can get my car fixed, at least.'

Angel sighed. 'Yes. If other people are here — ' she glanced across at Kyle, ' — we can't really stay, can we. It's like we're imposing.' It was a statement, rather than a question.

'Don't let me stop you,' said Kyle. 'Really and truly. You guys can hang on if you like. I'm more than happy to head home.'

Zac shook his head. 'You've got further to travel than us. It's more difficult to get a flight than a car fixed.'

'Hmm.' Kyle slid into a chair. 'It's big enough for us all, though.' His eyes drifted towards Angel, calculating, thinking about something. 'And there are a few things we need to discuss, Cousin Zac. And a few things I'd like to learn about the place before I leave. Shall we agree to disagree? Keep out of some people's way — ' at this, his eyes flashed angrily at Angel and she understood his meaning perfectly well, thank you very much ' — and we can see what happens tomorrow?'

'That sounds reasonable to me,' replied easy-going Zac. He grinned. 'What do you reckon, Angel?'

'Keeping out of the way sounds ideal,' she said.

14

Kyle watched out of the drawing room window as the recovery service guy disappeared again under the bonnet of Zac's car. He was onto his third cup of coffee. The Princess of Darkness had been right — he was like a bear with a sore head if he didn't have coffee in a morning. But that wasn't something he would admit to her.

Zac and he had got straight down to business after the makeshift breakfast. Angel had disappeared through the back door, muttering something about going for a walk, but he had seen the determined set of her chin and the whitened knuckles and clenched fists as she had swept out.

There was a considerable amount of head-scratching and conversation going on outside and Kyle hoped the car wasn't terminal, for his cousin's sake.

He turned away and headed back to the kitchen, washing his cup and peering out of the window above the sink, checking for a glimpse of Angel. If she was out of the picture, and Zac was busy with his car, there was something he wanted to do. There was a fleeting touch of black, threading through the trees towards the Loch — so unless the woman from his dream was wandering about out there, he was pretty safe as regards his plan.

That plan involved the tower room. He had looked at the estate agent's floorplan of the house along with the other paperwork during his conversation with Zac earlier, and he knew that odd little staircase on the landing would take him into a corridor which would then lead him along to the tower room. He had a strange feeling it would be the only place in Taigh Fallon that might resemble the place in his dream. And once he got in there, he hoped he would at least make some sense of that weird dream.

He remembered visiting the house as a child. More than that, he remembered Great Aunt Jeanie. He and Zac were allowed pretty much everywhere downstairs, but not really up. But, in the way of boys, he'd done his fair share of creeping around, and his more than fair share of telling Zac he couldn't follow him. Yeah. He maybe wasn't so proud of that attitude now.

So maybe he had been to that tower room then? It had been at least two decades ago, and real life had pushed many of those childhood memories out of his head. Maybe the dream last night had just been some of those old memories stirring. But he'd like to find out for sure.

The little staircase was polished oak, the handrail worn smooth from generations of people going up and down it towards, he guessed, the servants' quarters and the attics. It was not too big a leap to believe that servants had been housed here a few generations ago — a cook, a housekeeper, a maid or two; not a lot of people, but enough to assist with the general running of the place. Maybe a nanny or a footman or a groom — who knew? It was odd to think that so many lives had been played out under those grey slates. A memory nudged at him — *they didn't live in. She didn't want them watching her every move.*

The door at the top of the small staircase was unlatched and Kyle turned the handle, stepping into the quiet corridor. He paused for a moment, taking in the smell of old wood and varnish and beeswax that still lingered on the floorboards and turned to his left, walking along the corridor to an arched door that stood temptingly half-open.

Beyond the door, he heard a whispering. Muted conversation that meant nothing to him — the voices were to-ing and fro-ing as if arguing and he smiled wryly, wondering if the indistinct mutterings were drifting up from the courtyard where the recovery man was poking and prodding at Zac's car.

Unfazed, Kyle pushed the door open and the conversation stopped abruptly. There was faint scent of rosewater and lilies; a breath on his neck as something invisible slipped past him and drifted down the corridor. He turned quickly, instinctively, and saw a shadow diffuse along the corridor. The skin on the back of his neck prickled and he spun back towards the room.

It was identical to the one in his dream, right down to the three windows and the rain-drenched castle ruins on the west; right down to the oval mirror and the spindly-legged table and the faded velvet upholstery on the chairs.

He must, he reasoned, looking around him, have been here when he was younger. It would have been the ideal place for a game of hide and seek, the perfect secret place to huddle up and count to one hundred in the little room beyond —

He looked at the fireplace and

spotted the empty bookshelves either side of it.

The one on the left. That was the one he needed.

As if in the dream again, Kyle walked over to the fireplace and stood in front of the bookshelves. His gaze scoured the shelves until he saw it — the tiniest of levers, right at the top. His heart beating fast, he reached up and touched it. Something sprang into life and there was a creak as the whole bookshelf jolted out of the wall and turned slightly.

'Good God,' he murmured and took hold of the edge of the casing. Pulling it towards him, the thing transformed into a door that swung around in a half circle, revealing a little wood-panelled room and a spiral staircase heading downwards. This was something the estate agent had missed.

Kyle was a sensible man, and he didn't go into that room immediately. He stepped out, back into the tower room and grabbed a chair. He wedged the chair in the doorway, just in case it decided to swing back and trap him there. It might only be a tiny room, some sort of secret folly — and there must be a way out down the stairs — but who knew if the exit would even be accessible now?

Kyle walked back into the tower room and peered down the stairs. Even as he stood there, his memory refused to co-operate as to anything else about that place. It may have been that he had hid there as a child after all, but . . .

Another cold shiver ran down his back. There was the small matter of the secret lever being so high up and well-hidden that a man of over six foot had to reach up and touch it before it moved.

Realistically, how could a kid playing hide and seek have discovered that?

★   ★   ★

Angel had walked down to the water's edge again. The rain had turned into a light drizzle that morning, and now had stopped completely. It was still rather dull and overcast, but the place looked a lot less forbidding in daylight. A few weak rays of sun were trying gamely to brighten up the ruined castle and Angel thought how beautiful it would be in full sunlight.

The formal gardens were behind her, the pebbles of the paths made shiny by the rain, and she picked up a stone from the shore, listlessly skimming it across the Loch. She knew it was sensible, and perhaps expected, for Zac and Kyle to sell Taigh Fallon and split the money, as she could see no real reason for either of them keeping it. Zac's life was on Skye and he wasn't that enamoured of the mainland; Kyle, presumably, lived and worked in Canada. But still, what a shame. She would have loved the opportunity to spend a little more time here, but in her heart of hearts she understood that she'd been lucky to have the time that she'd had.

Angel sat down on the trunk of a

fallen tree, not caring that it was still damp from the rain. She was determined to let the peace of this place wash over her. If she treated it like a little holiday, that would be good. Go back to Skye with Zac today, probably, and spend tomorrow up there; then travel back to Whitby in time for the weekend trade. She'd have no ghost stories for Grace, though, but a man like Kyle Fallon creeping around a darkened house was probably worse . . .

'Daylight! And you. Oh well. With light comes shadow, as they say.' Kyle had appeared from, it seemed, nowhere. He was dishevelled and dusty and furious, brushing himself down.

'And sometimes people arriving to disrupt the peace are even worse.' She stood up. 'I'm going back to the house.'

'Ha! Which way?' He nodded back the way he had come. 'That way?'

Angel followed his glance. 'There's nothing that way. The house is back up the steps.'

'That's one way back. Or you can go

through the ice house.'

'The *ice* house?' Angel stared at him. 'But ice houses are just ice houses. Holes in the ground. Giant freezers.'

'Usually,' replied Kyle. 'Unless they're an exit from a corridor into the house. Which that one over there appears to be.' He flicked some more dust off his shoulders, letting Angel process the information.

'Where does it go?'

'The tower room. Along to a staircase and up.'

'So that's how you got in last night! I knew it.'

'Last night? I used the front door last night! I have a key, remember.'

'Well, I'm pretty sure I saw you in the tower room.'

'And I'm pretty sure I told you that I knew nothing about that corridor! And I was damn well not in that tower room.'

'So you're going to tell me it's a secret corridor for smugglers or something? And you just happened to stumble on it today?'

'No! Don't be ridiculous. It was probably a short cut for whoever collected the ice. There's probably an entrance in the corridor branching off to the kitchens — but there is definitely an entrance to the tower — ' he balled his fists and flung his arms wide ' — for *whatever* reason.'

He looked like a big, crouching raven at that moment, and Angel was a little disturbed to feel a stirring of something like admiration creep up her spine. She quickly shook it off.

'And I *did* just find it today,' he continued. 'Believe what you want.' It was his turn to stride off towards the steps, leaving Angel standing on the shore with the waves lapping at her feet, wondering whether she dared go towards this mythical ice house and see this corridor for herself.

15

Angel, being Angel, decided to do just that. She watched Kyle disappear into the woods, waited until the trees had swallowed him up, then walked over to the rocks he had appeared from.

At first glance, she realised, they had appeared to be a tumble of rocks, but as she drew closer she saw that it was a roughly shaped mound covered in grass and overgrown foliage; the ice house, cleverly disguised as part of the scenery. She smiled, understanding that the Fallons of yore who had built this place had, as so many other families had, wanted the day-to-day activity of the house and the less pleasant aspects of it all banished from view. Had they been entertaining guests on the little pebbled shore — perhaps the gentlemen fishing whilst the ladies sat around a cast iron table and gossiped over tea and buns

— they would have wanted the servants well out of view. They would have wanted the fact that the ice for their summer sorbets or their bottles of champagne came from a hole in the ground, full of God knows what, hidden away.

There was a wooden door on a rusted hinge firmly closed and she took the handle in both hands, ready to heave it open. Surprisingly, it opened reasonably easily. Kyle must have had the tougher job of easing it away from the doorway as he pushed against it from inside.

Angel peered into the gloom, her eyes adjusting to the dark, green light filtering through, she assumed, some cracks in the old brickwork. She stepped in and felt along the wall, the smell of damp and decay creeping into her nostrils. She shuddered as she imagined how easy it would be to fall into the deep cavernous hole she was sure was before her, and never be found.

'Ugh,' she said, for no other reason than hearing the sound of her own voice. 'G-g-g' repeated an echo, her words bouncing of the walls and she shivered.

As her eyes adjusted, she saw a walkway going around the side of the pit, and realised this was where Kyle had come from. It stretched out beyond her, a faint phosphorescence, almost, glowing as though inviting her forwards. There must be windows or skylights, she reasoned — not just cracks in the brickwork. After all, if *he* had managed to walk around it safely, there must be enough light to see by.

She couldn't quite make herself walk on though. The idea of being stuck in there, without a light, and the door slamming shut behind her creeped her out.

But was she really going to let Kyle Fallon have all the fun? No.

She didn't stop to think it through more deeply. He had come out. The tower room was beyond her. It was fine.

She did, however, nip back outside and get the biggest stones she could muster, piling them up around the entrance so the door had no way of slamming shut and trapping her in there.

Once she was happy with the barrier, she headed into the ice house, hugging the wall, walking carefully on the rough, uneven stonework. There was a handrail around the edge of the pit, and, she knew, a ladder would lead down into the ground. However, she didn't trust the handrail and didn't fancy her chances with the ladder, so hugging the wall was the best, and safest, option.

Angel picked her way around the pit, her heart pounding as she travelled further into the darkness. Eventually she stood at the entrance to the real corridor and saw it snaking away in front of her, lit by that weird greenish glow. There was nothing for it but to walk along it.

Holding her hands out and touching the wall, Angel inched her way along the corridor. The few minutes she was in there, walking into spiders' webs and crunching through dead leaves and twigs, seriously felt like an hour. At the end of the corridor, she came to a small fork. One way, she guessed, would take her into the kitchens of the house; the other would take her to the tower. She pivoted around and tried to imagine Kyle standing here, focused as he was on the pale light up ahead spotting the corridor, she could understand why he had missed the turning into the kitchens. That would have been on his left as he stood here. It gave her a little thrill of envy and annoyance to think that man had been here less than half an hour ago. He was the one who had disturbed the layers of dust, the particles of which danced and floated so thickly around her in the half-light, that she could almost taste them.

Determinedly, she turned around again and reached out for the door a little way in front of her. There was a loud creak and it swung back, revealing what seemed to be a different world.

Angel's eyes widened as she stepped

into a small, square, wood-panelled hall-way. There was scuffed parquet flooring beneath her feet and an ancient, cracked blue and white jug on a shelf in an alcove. She guessed that at one time, the jug might have held flowers and blinked, trying to imagine what the place might have looked like. Ahead of her, was the beginning of a spiral staircase, a blotched and spotted mirror hanging above the archway that led to the stairs. The little hallway smelled old and damp, the stone stairs not even worn into little crescents, not telling tales of hundreds of feet traipsing up and down them over the years. The staircase was not, then, another servants' staircase.

There was a flicker of anticipation and a half-remembered feeling of loss prickling Angel's skin. A cool breath, almost like a sigh, brushed the back of her neck and she instinctively raised her hand to bat whatever it was away. She caught sight of a dark shape, just next to her, reflected in the ancient mirror.

Something like cold fingers fastened

around her wrist and slipped up her hand, wrapping itself around her own fingers. She couldn't help it; she screamed and bolted forwards, up the steps, two at a time.

★　★　★

Thank God that the door was open into the tower room. *Thank God, thank God, thank God.*

Angel dived into the room and spun around. Somebody, probably Kyle, had propped the door open with a chair. She grabbed the chair and yanked it away from the entrance, sending it careering across the floor.

There was a sort of triple *slam* as the tower room door shut, a bookcase to her right snapped back into place, and the main door to the room flew open.

A shadow fell across Angel, the bulk of someone filling the doorway, his fury palpable. 'I thought you'd come in here. You couldn't resist it, could you?'

Angel opened her mouth to scream

again, when the bulk stepped into the tower room and revealed itself as Kyle. Abruptly, she snapped her mouth shut. Her shock came out in a strangely gurgling, strangled-sounding gulp.

He strode up to her and towered over her. 'Do you realise how stupid that was? Did you even think that I might have locked the door back up? Did you even consider the fact you might be stuck in that damn corridor?'

The man was raging at her and Angel stared at him, waiting for him to pause before she gathered the energy to shout back at him.

It was no good though. She just had to shout over the top of him. 'But I *wouldn't* have been stuck in it! I wedged the ice house door open; there are *two* doors down there and one would have led into the house downstairs. *You* — ' here she pointed a black-tipped finger at him ' — wedged this door open anyway. And if all else failed, you've just admitted that you knew where I'd be!'

'That's beside the point,' he almost

roared. He grabbed her shoulders, bringing his face down, quite close to hers. She could see the bronze flecks in his dark brown eyes and felt her body responding in a way she didn't like.

Despite the way she arched slightly towards him and tilted her head up, her lips parting, inches from his, she pulled herself up short and stiffened. 'Don't even *pretend* you care about what happens to me.' She shook him off and ducked away, her cheeks flaring. 'I don't know how you found the entrance up here, but it'll be pretty easy for me to find the one at the ice house again.'

She stormed out of the tower room, her dress rustling angrily and slammed the door behind her.

1897

He watched her leave. They had come too close again — too close for the sake of propriety. He turned and slammed his hand into the bookshelf, echoing the door, punching out his frustration. He stood back, pushing his hair away from his forehead. Then he leaned forward and rested his head against the spines of the books, inhaling the scent of old leather and printing ink, feeling the coolness take away some of his anger.

Connor. He'd never leave his guilt behind. It would haunt him forever.

He turned and faced the mirror. 'What do you see, my angel?' he murmured. He wondered if she had been there again, watching them; watching Annis's increasingly pathetic and desperate attempts to contact her husband. He walked over and leaned in towards the glass. She flickered into view, perplexed. Her background was different; dark and hemmed in. She looked lost, confused. He reached out his hand, wanting, strangely, to touch her; expecting only to caress the smooth surface again.

Yet this time: this time, his hand slipped through the glass as if it was water. Ripples surrounded his wrist as it sunk further in towards her. Her wrist was there, raised up, those strange patterns etched on her milk-white skin. If he leaned a little further, he could almost encircle it. His heart beating fast, his fingers closed around hers.

She whipped her hand away and faded.

As if stung, he pulled his hand back, clenched still into a fist. He unfurled it, sweat breaking out on his skin as he realised he was not empty-handed.

A jet ring lay in his palm, studded with diamonds in the shape of a flower. It glinted in a weak patch of sunlight and he found he could not look away.

16

Kyle stared after her, looking at the door which was now firmly shut against the outside world. His flesh crawled as he thought of her trapped in that corridor, and of course the thought was ridiculous. She had been right — no way would she ever have been stuck in there.

He wasn't sure what had alerted him to the fact she would emerge from that spiral staircase at that precise point in time. All he knew was that he was downstairs, washing the worst of the grime and dust off his hands when he stiffened, his head snapping upright.

'Annis.'

The voice was as clear as anything, an uncomfortable reminder of his dream.

'No!' he yelled, and ran out of the kitchen, taking the oak staircase two at a time and bursting in just as she was shoving the chair across the floor. She looked incongruous, yet not. Her clothes seemed to fit in with the age of the tower room, but her attitude most certainly did not.

He hadn't been able to stop himself. Images of her stuck in there, shouting for help, banging on the doors assaulted his mind. He was crazy. Absolutely crazy. And of course, there she was, yelling back at him, pressing so close that he could feel the heat from her body, see the individual lashes that framed her dark eyes.

He was pleased she had pulled away before instinct took over and he pulled her closer. Then, he guessed, they would both have been lost.

1897

She locked herself away in her room, sitting heavily on the edge of her bed. He was so close, just out of sight. She had to keep trying. Today she had almost reached him, she was convinced. Then, as she stood in the tower room, she had become all too aware of Alasdair before her, the air crackling between them with that animal lust which had driven their actions so heinously almost eight months ago.

The spring day was pressing in on her, the room airless and too warm, surely, for the time of year. She caught sight of herself in the mirror. Twenty-two years old, she looked twice that. Her cheekbones stood out, too sharp, her eyes shadowed and as black as her gown. She smoothed the skirts down, the tiny jet beads pricking her fingers. The dress was unwieldy and uncomfortable, too many layers and too much weight for her small frame. As the child grew within her, it was a constant cycle of tightening fabric and loosening seams. It wouldn't be long now — she ran her hand beneath her stomach. Hard and smooth beneath the folds of fabric, she wondered how much more her body would have to change. Five weeks, she reckoned. In five weeks it would be over with.

She told herself the child would look like Connor. It would have his eyes.

She couldn't let herself believe it was Alasdair's eyes that would stare back at her.

The guilt, she thought, would never leave her. As oppressive as this room, the hell she had created for herself would eventually close in and swallow her up.

Sometimes, she hoped it would happen sooner rather than later.

★ ★ ★

Angel fled through the house until she was at the front door; then she ran out and went to find Zac. He was lurking around the corner, staring at his 4x4 quite miserably.

He turned as he heard her coming and frowned. 'It's not looking good,' he said morosely. 'It needs some parts. It could take a good few hours to get them. They have to go and source them or something.' He waved his hand dismissively. 'Whatever it is, I can't go anywhere fast.'

Angel had mixed feelings about that. Part of her desperately wanted to stay at the house, and part of her wanted to be as far away from Kyle Fallon as possible.

With a bit of an effort, she quashed down her own feelings and patted Zac on the arm. 'At least it's not terminal,' she said. 'You'll soon be back on Skye. Have you told Ivy yet?'

Zac shook his head. 'I need to call her. She'll be waiting for me.'

'Then call her. And while you've got the phone, call your bloody solicitor and get your bloody cousin disinherited.'

'What?' Zac stared at her. 'You can't be serious, Angel. I'm not going to do that!'

Angel sighed. 'I *know*, Zac. But I wish you *could* do that. He's very obnoxious.' Then: 'Oh hell! Look. *Look*, Zac.' She lifted up her hand, the one she'd been resting on his arm. 'My ring's come off. How annoying. I put that on especially for Jeanie.' She raised her eyes heavenwards and called out: 'I'm sorry, Jeanie! I wore it to give you the utmost respect. My intentions were true, I promise!'

Zac caught her hand and studied it. 'Do you think it broke?'

'I have no idea. But staring at my hand won't help us. Unless you're staring because you fancy a tattoo?' She wiggled her wrist within his grasp until he let her hand drop.

'No thanks. I don't do pain and anguish.'

'It wasn't really that painful. And anyway, I like it.'

'It *is* pretty,' Zac admitted, 'but definitely something more suited to you and not to me.'

'Yeah, I know. Look — phone Ivy, would you? Tell her you'll be delayed today as well. I'm sure she'll be fine about it.' Zac dropped his gaze and she saw his hand creep into his pocket.

He withdrew his phone and held it up. 'I'll call her,' he said. 'Anything to get you off my back.'

'Good.' She nodded. 'Oh, but before you do, did you know you had a secret corridor at this place? That's what I came to tell you.' Zac's easy-going nature had at least dissipated the feelings she'd had in that tower room and she already felt calmer.

'A secret corridor?' Zac stared at her. 'You sure you haven't been at Jeanie's whisky?'

'I was at it last night, as you well know,' she said, grinning, 'but no. I'm sober as a judge now and I swear to you there's a corridor. Just ask Mr Happy.'

'Ask Mr Happy what?' The smooth Canadian voice was far too close. She felt her cheeks grow hot and his breath warmed her ear. 'And who,' he continued, even more smoothly, 'is Mr Happy?'

Angel chose not to answer the second question.

Instead, she turned slowly towards him. 'I'm telling Zac about the secret corridor. The one from the tower room. I'm sure he's entitled to know about it.'

'I'm sure he is. And if he's going to explore it, I'm sure he would be sensible enough to tell someone he was going to do that.'

'Yes. I'm sure he would. But it's not really necessary to do that, is it, when somebody else has already been stupid enough to try it first — '

'Okay, okay,' said Zac. 'I haven't a clue what you're both talking about, but I am interested in the secret corridor. Where is it exactly?'

It seemed as if the idea of the corridor had perked Zac up and made him forget the fact he was stranded on the mainland — which was an ironic way of looking at the situation.

Angel folded her arms and studied her friend. 'I'm saying nothing until you call Ivy,' she said. 'After *that*, you can see the corridor.'

'Ivy? I'm still stuck on the mainland.' Zac pulled a face. 'They need parts for the car. They said it could be a few hours. They're going to tow it to the garage.'

'A few hours? Will you get back tonight then?'

'I'm hoping to. But I've got a problem. I don't feel right leaving Angel here but I don't think she wants to come back to Skye just yet. She'd love a few more days but there's stuff going on.'

'Oh! Is there anything I can do?' Ivy sounded concerned and Zac smiled, thinking of her furrowing her brows.

'Not unless you come here and save Angel's soul from eternal damnation.'

'What?' This time she sounded shocked.

'Well, it's just that my cousin's turned up from Canada. He was left part of the house as well — it's pretty complicated, but it appears that Angel and Kyle don't get on very well. Actually, they don't get on at all. I think she's going to murder him before long. I can tell.'

'Really? What do you mean by 'don't get on'?'

'They argue. *Constantly*. She really hates him.'

'Hate is a strong word, Zac.' She sounded amused.

'Believe me. It's truly hate.'

'Hmm. You know what they say, though, don't you?'

'No. What?'

'Hate is very close to love.'

Zac laughed. 'Wheesht! There's no way that's on the cards! It's like a battle of words and wills the whole time. They've only had about twelve hours in each other's company as well.'

'Aye.' There was another pause. 'I suppose that's not the way for everyone, but it suits some people. I think it's called passion. *Wuthering Heights* and all that.'

'Seriously? I couldn't be bothered

with all that. They're a pair, all right — both as black as the Earl of Hell's waistcoat! But it wouldn't be for me.'

'What *could* you be bothered with, then, Zac?' Her voice was amused.

Zac stared at the phone. It was a very good question. He opened his mouth to reply, then closed it again.

The moment was lost, though, as Ivy spoke. 'Oh — some post came today.' There was a rustle and a clatter as she put the phone down to, presumably, sort the post out. 'It's from the solicitor, I think. It's a truly official looking envelope.'

'I'll get it when I come back. It's probably to tell me they've located Kyle.'

'I think, from what you say, you located him first.'

'He located Taigh Fallon before that. And now — ' Zac looked over his shoulder ' — I can hear them arguing about the secret corridor. Again.'

'Secret corridor?'

'Apparently we have one. Kyle found it, Angel went in afterwards, and I think they are both trying to lay claim to it. Or they might be complaining about the fact that each one of them has been in it without the other one's permission. Or perhaps they just want to brick each other up in it.'

'It sounds very much like they don't know what they want with anything.'

'You're probably right. Anyway, I'm sorry I won't be back. Can you manage for another day if you need to?'

'I'm sure I can, but there's something I need to talk to you about when you do get back.'

'Okay. Do I need to worry?'

'Ha! No, not too much. It's just I've got the chance to go back to Glastonbury sooner than I thought, and I'm considering doing it. It just means that you'll need a new assistant quite quickly, if I do go.'

'Oh. Right. I kind of thought it wasn't so — imminent.'

'It wasn't meant to be, but the chance has come up for a studio. I have to take it.'

'I suspect you do. But you won't be gone by tomorrow, will you? So I'll still see you then, aye?'

'Aye.'

Zac looked up at the blue sky breaking out over Eilean Donan and frowned at nothing in particular, thinking about his car. 'That's if I get back. Right. I'll call you tomorrow, okay, and let you know what's happening. If it's too late, Angel will just force me to stay another night anyway.'

'The place isn't going to run away,' replied Ivy. There was still a smile in her voice.

'No,' said Zac. 'It's not.'

17

Angel took Zac to the corridor, as she promised.

'It goes all the way through to the tower room,' she said as they peered into the ice house entrance.

'But it's not recommended to travel within the corridor, unless you have clear access in and out,' added the Canadian voice beside her. 'And I don't know if you've actually got that, have you? Do you even know how to open the door up there?'

Kyle had, of course, decided to come along; primarily, Angel suspected, to annoy her.

'Well it's just as well there are three of us. You can either stay outside to make sure we don't get lost, or go away and open it up yourself. Come on, Zac. I'll take you through.' She took hold of his arm and stepped into the entrance.

'It's safe enough to go up the staircase.'

'So it's just into the tower room?' Zac stared around him. 'It's an odd place to carry ice into.'

'It's not just the tower room,' replied Angel. 'There's another corridor that branches off to the kitchens, I think. I haven't explored that one yet.'

'That surprises me. You seem to be in the habit of wandering through corridors and into rooms with no idea what could be in them.' Yes, Kyle was definitely on a mission to annoy her. It didn't help that he sounded amused and she was beginning to suspect he was doing it just to get a reaction from her.

'At least I make sure I'm in company when I do it,' responded Angel. 'I don't just attempt it randomly.'

'And we're back to that, are we?' asked Kyle, although it was very clear that he did not require an answer.

'I don't think we can come to that much grief by attempting the entrance into the kitchen,' continued Angel. 'It's probably the better corridor of the two. I suspect people would have used it more.'

'Well I'm up for it if you are,' replied Zac.

'Of course I am,' she answered warmly. 'This way.' Somehow she managed to get in front of them all and walked ahead, pointing out the great hole beside them where the ice would have been kept.

She was gratified to hear Zac sound impressed.

'Definitely a good place to hide a body.' His voice echoed around the chamber. 'I've read books and seen plenty of TV shows where they do that. There are always a set of bleached bones hanging around.'

'I hope there aren't any left in here though!' said Angel. 'I don't think I want any skeletons to jump out at me.'

'Yet you say you aren't scared of ghosts,' teased Zac.

Angel laughed. 'I'm not scared of ghosts. The dead can't hurt you. But skeletons . . . ugh. They were covered in skin once upon a time. And they *rattle* at you. Ugh.'

There was a Canadian-sounding snort which may have disguised a laugh. Angel couldn't help it. She dipped her head down and allowed herself a small smile. He had a sense of humour, of sorts, then.

'Anyway,' she continued, 'this is the junction where it splits. If you go left, you head up into the tower room. And if you go right, this is where we assume it goes into the kitchens.'

She paused and looked at the studded wooden door in front of her. 'I think it'll be okay just to open it. The other one was fine.' She took hold of the handle and tugged with all her might. Something splintered and creaked above her and she looked up.

The door moved slowly at first. Then she realised that it wasn't so much opening as falling, coming away from its hinges and coming closer to her. It all seemed to happen very quickly. The huge wooden door fell in a plume of dust and dirt and spider-webs, and a pair of strong arms grabbed her around the waist and pulled her away from it. The door landed about six inches away from her and she was frozen to the spot, staring at the broken wood and coughing at the dust which rose around her. Even so, she was more than aware of the grip around her waist, the heat of his skin through the fabric of her bodice.

'Like I keep telling you,' he murmured in her ear, his voice tight, 'it's not safe down here. Are you going to damage yourself, just to prove me wrong?'

She turned to him, her mouth partially open as she prepared to answer. His face was very close to hers, the warmth of his breath on her skin. His mouth, parted as hers was, moving closer —

'Angel!' Zac shouted her name, scrambling through the debris and coughing his way through the dust. 'Good grief! Are you okay?'

He appeared next to her, and all at

once Angel was embarrassed. She felt particularly stupid, having persuaded her friend to come down here, assuring him it was fine, confidently proclaiming the kitchen corridor was safe . . .

'God! I'm sorry Zac. I've killed your house.' She shifted position and Kyle's hands dropped away. She was aware of him stepping to the side, melting into the shadows of the corridor.

'No! No you haven't killed it. It's just rotten wood. The rooms beyond will be fine, I'm sure.'

Angel shook her head. 'No. I don't want to chance it.' She pressed herself against the wall. 'I'd never forgive myself if something happened to you.'

'Why don't you stick to what you know?' Kyle spoke softly but firmly. 'You can take Zac up to the tower where we know it's safe and I'll go back and open the door up. The place needs a proper survey before you go tramping through any more corridors.'

'All right.' Annoyingly, her voice was quavering. The falling door must have

163

shaken her more than she realised. 'Zac?'

'Only if you want to.' He shrugged and stared behind him. 'I don't want to force you.'

She followed his gaze. She thought she saw one of the shadows on the wall break away and move towards the entrance, but she blinked and the illusion vanished. 'No, no. It's your house. It's whatever you want to do.' She wrapped her arms around herself. 'I think I'm probably taking over a bit — like it's my place. But it's yours. Yours and Kyle's. I'm sorry.'

Zac turned back to her, surprised. 'I never thought you were taking over. You're just showing me some of its secrets, that's all.' He looked around him. 'It doesn't even *feel* like my house. I liked it when I was a kid, but I liked Jeanie more. I enjoyed her visiting us, more than coming here. It always felt a bit — big. I don't know what you think, Kyle?'

'Now I'm back, it feels pretty homely

to me,' replied Kyle, frankly. 'I remember bits and pieces from when I was a kid. I always loved it, loved coming here to visit Jeanie. I even loved how creepy it was, if I'm honest. But I was a bit older.' His gaze slid away as something flickered across his face, then slid back. 'And I'm sorry I treated you like I did — I have to get that out there. But I feel happy here, in some ways. Then I guess I'm unsettled in others. It's weird.'

'Think nothing of it. We were children. And you were the older child. It happens.' Zac shrugged. 'But as far as Taigh Fallon itself goes, I have no wish to keep it. I was never meant for the mainland. It's not my home. I wish I could just hand it over to you guys. I can tell how much you both love it.' He laughed and shook his head. 'There you have it. Who would reject a place like this, except daft old me? Aye. Daft.' This time, he nodded. 'Now. Are you going to take me up to this tower room?'

'Yes. I will, if you want to go.' Angel

peeled herself away from the wall. 'Seriously, just tell me if I'm out of order though.'

'I always do,' replied Zac.

★ ★ ★

Kyle watched Angel and Zac head back along the corridor and turn sharply towards the tower entrance. He wondered how long they'd been together.

They seemed as if they knew each other pretty well, but he couldn't quite get his head around what actually *kept* them together. They were complete opposites; his cousin was laid-back and easy-going — and she was anything but. Perhaps the bond was the creative side of them? Kyle had gathered his cousin now lived and worked on Skye, designing and making jewellery. Angel did much the same thing in Whitby, from what he understood, thanks to some chat with Zac over the breakfast table, before the guy had come for Zac's car. And Zac's job, he thought, was a world away from his. Although maybe there was still a creative aspect to his, in some ways.

Taking into account the distance between Skye and Whitby, that was another interesting thing about their relationship: how they maintained it. He half-smiled, watching the corner they had disappeared around. Perhaps she was just easier to love at a distance. Regardless, he waited for a moment, just in case any more near-disasters befell them, before he headed back out to the Loch side.

Kyle broke into a run as he made his way through the gardens, wanting to make sure the door really was open into the tower room for them when they appeared. The voices were there again, whispering insistently behind the door, until he flung it open and was greeted by silence. He strode over to the bookshelf and touched the lever, watching the door spring open. He could hear their voices coming up the stairs; Zac's, low and amused, Angel's, higher pitched and excitable. She was laughing about something, but he didn't know what. She'd obviously recovered her humour.

He walked back into the room, waiting for them, and went over to the mirror. He stared at himself and wondered when a scowl had become *de rigeur* for his facial expression. Probably, he reasoned, since he had come to Taigh Fallon and locked horns with Angel Tempest.

As he studied his face and ran his hand over the stubble on his chin, she appeared in the mirror behind him. 'Oh, you made it, then,' he said and turned around. The words died on his lips as he realised he was still alone in the room. 'Angel? Zac?'

They burst through from the little hallway, Angel in the lead, laughing over her shoulder at Zac. 'See? I told you it led right back here. Oh. Kyle. Hello.' She stopped, wrong-footed slightly, apparently not expecting him to be waiting for them. 'Anyway. Like I said, Zac, this corridor is just one of Taigh Fallon's secrets. We'll have to sort the kitchen one out. Oh.' Her face fell. 'No. No, we won't. It's nothing to do with me and you don't really care, do you?'

Kyle looked away, at the door behind her, where they'd appeared. She might not be able to sort the corridor out; his cousin might not *want* to sort the corridor out. Personally speaking, he felt it would just be better all round if the bloody thing was blocked up permanently. He looked at Angel and felt his face settle into a scowl again. If it was blocked up, it would prevent her wandering through it at any rate.

It would keep her safe.

He shuddered. That time, the voice had sounded very close to his ear.

1897

Helpless, he stood in the corner as she lit more candles, thumbed through more books, following the text with her fingers, murmuring strange incantations.

'Please. Just stop,' he said. 'Stop this, Annis.'

Her eyes never leaving the book she studied, she shook her head. 'No.'

'For God's sake. What do you want to do?' He snapped, at long last. 'Dredge it all up again? What do you hope to prove?'

'There is nothing to prove.' Her voice was measured. 'You said so yourself, when it happened. I want to talk to my husband.' Her hand brushed her dress, resting against her stomach. 'I want to tell him about his child.'

'Annis!'

'It is Connor's child.' Her answer was curt.

'Connor had an illness when he was younger — they said he could not — '

Annis swung round, her eyes glittering. 'That is not true. It is his child.'

Alasdair pushed his hand through his hair, turning away from her and striding to the window.

He leaned on the windowsill and rested his head on the glass, the pulse pounding in his temples. 'It's not Connor's child. And all our family know it cannot be his. What do you think they will say when it is born? What do you think they are saying now? I should not spend so long here, but it is the only option. I can't abandon you to their displeasure. I can perhaps convince them the doctors were wrong if the child looks like my brother in any way at all.'

'You lie to me. Sit down.'

'No.'

'Sit down!'

'No!'

'Sit down! I — ' There was a gasp and a clatter as a candlestick fell and skittered across the floor. The candle had been lit, and a scorch mark trailed after it before the flame guttered.

Alasdair spun around. She was leaning on the table, one hand clutching the edge of it, the other pressed to her stomach.

'I — ' she repeated, her face even paler than before. 'Alasdair...'

'I'm here, I'm here.' In an instant he

was with her, his arms around her, supporting her as she leaned into him sobbing.

'Help me,' she whispered. 'Help me. Stay with me. Please. I think it's time.'

'I won't leave you,' he murmured into her hair.

He guided her into the chair and looked up, catching sight of the mirror; wondering, even now, if his dark angel was there. Annis was unaware of her — she always had been, it seemed. But it was to the angel he now began to pray: Let all be well, let all be well.

18

The sun had come out again and the spring air was fresh and clean, so they had decided to take lunch into the gardens; well, at least Zac and Angel had. Kyle had made an excuse, and unpacked a laptop. He'd set it up in a small room off the dining room, which was a perfect little place for a study.

Well, Angel would have made it into a study, at least. She would have a bigger room as a workshop, or even maybe one of those outbuildings at the back of the house that looked out over the Loch and the gardens. Stables or sheds; she wasn't quite certain what they had been, but she could envisage them full of her jet and her equipment.

She let out a small sigh and Zac looked at her. 'What?' he asked. 'What are you thinking about?'

'Taigh Fallon. Living here. How nice

it would be.' She scanned the grounds and her gaze settled on the house. 'Jeanie was a lucky woman. Do you think she knew all of its secrets? Do you think she knew about the tower room and the corridor?'

'Probably. More than we know, at any rate. She lived here all her life, remember.'

'And we've been here for a day and already found the corridor. I think that's pretty good.'

'Who knows what else you'll discover if we're stuck here any longer. I — oh!' He looked down as his mobile phone rang in his pocket. 'Hello? Oh! Hello. Aye. That's me. *The garage*,' he mouthed to Angel, gesturing to the phone. 'You've got the part? Oh, that's great. Thanks.' He grinned. 'Aye. Thanks.' There was a little more conversation, the gist of which was that the car would be finished and delivered later that same day. 'That's good news, isn't it?' said Zac. 'I can probably get back home tonight. You can come as well.'

'But what's the point of that?' Angel hoped she didn't sound as desperate as she thought she did. 'Can't we stay on just one more day? Please? It could be late. You'll need to be very well rested to drive safely.'

Zac looked at her curiously. 'What *is* it about this place, Angel? What is it that makes you want to hang on?'

'I have no idea,' replied Angel honestly. 'You know when you just get a feeling about a place? It's like that.'

'A feeling about a place?' teased Zac. 'Not a feeling about a person?'

Angel looked back at the house and up at the tower room. A shadow of a person filled the window. It might well have been Kyle, taking a break from his work and having a wander up there.

Angel believed that, until she saw a second shadow next to the first one. She pointed to the window, about to comment, when a man came around the corner.

'Thought I'd break for coffee and come out to join you guys,' said Kyle.

Angel looked at him, and their eyes met briefly, a flash of something in his before he slid his gaze away and went to sit next to his cousin on the garden wall. 'Hey, Zac, can we talk later? In private?'

Angel, biting back a sarcastic retort for Zac's sake, looked back at the tower room, and the shadows had gone.

★   ★   ★

After lunch, Angel disappeared to her bedroom. She sat on the bed and wondered whether she should start packing at all. Poor Zac — she hoped the car wouldn't be fixed until later, but she knew he would be wishing otherwise.

Her mobile phone was on the dressing table and looked incongruous somehow, in the old house amongst the vintage furniture. She spotted the light blinking and leaned forward, plucking it off the lace doily that covered the polished surface. A missed call from Jessie, her bookish sister. Angel smiled. She didn't mind Jessie interrupting her thoughts.

She pressed the button to call her back and Jessie answered almost immediately. 'Angel? I have the most amazing book for you. All about Victorian mourning traditions and *memento mori* and stuff. Right up your street.'

Angel pulled a face. 'And good afternoon to you too, sister. But *memento mori*? Horrid habit.' The idea of the Victorians taking photographs of dead people had never really appealed to Angel. Yes, she had rather a strange fascination for many Victorian customs, but that one made her flesh creep. It was very much at odds with her image, and she well knew that. But to her, it felt disrespectful.

'You'll still enjoy looking at the pictures,' said Jessie and Angel could hear the grin in her voice. 'Can I bring it over for you? If nothing else, it'll look good on the workshop mantelpiece.'

'You can bring it over, but I'm not at home. I'm in Scotland with Zac.'

'Oh! You never said. How's Skye? Stormy?'

'Possibly. I wouldn't know. We're on the mainland. His great aunt left him a house and I volunteered to come over with him to check it out. I can see Eilean Donan from my bedroom window.' She sounded wistful and she knew it. Her gaze travelled to the window and she stood up, walking over to see the view better. 'But yes,' she stared out at the ruins of the castle, dappled pink and gold now from the sunlight, 'the book would be great. I'll get it when I come back.'

'No problem. And when will that be?'

'Ha!' Angel laughed, mirthlessly. 'Much depends on many things. Whether Zac's car gets fixed. Whether we head back today or tomorrow. Whether Zac finishes whatever interesting conversation he's having with Kyle, because good grief, they look intent.' She rested the phone in the crook of her neck and fumbled with the window latch, throwing her weight behind it, shoving the casement open. It resisted a little, but not for long.

'Kyle?' asked Jessie. 'Do we know a Kyle?'

'Unfortunately, we do.'

It's for you to consider. The offer's on the table.

His voice carried, quite clearly through the gardens.

I've got a lot of experience, modernising these places. Check out my company, couz. It's worth thinking about. Hell, I've razed them to the ground before if the land's worth more than the building. Sometimes you have to make that decision, you know?

Aye. Thanks. That was Zac, sounding relieved. *I'll most certainly consider it.*

'Jessie, I have to go. I need to Google something on my phone.' Angel's heart was thumping. 'I love you. I'll call you when I get back, okay?' She didn't wait for an answer, cutting her sister off as if she was dead-heading a rose.

She turned her attention to Google, and typed in Kyle's name. What she saw on the screen made her eyes widen and the bile rise in her throat.

Kyle Fallon, International Property Developer, Ontario.

Restoration, Renovation and Clean-Cut Design Choices.

'How could you?' Angel shouted. She tossed the phone on the bed in a temper. She was annoyed at both of them — but especially bloody Kyle Fallon. She didn't know what he had planned for the place, but she was willing to bet that the corridors wouldn't come out of it well.

If her attitude had even been *slightly* softening towards him, the barriers were back up now, big-time.

19

Angel played that conversation between Zac and Kyle over and over. There was still only one conclusion she could come up with. Zac didn't want this place and Kyle had offered to take it off his hands.

'Angel?' There was a knock on the bedroom door and she went over to open it. Zac stood there, smiling ironically. 'My car. The garage has confirmed that it's being fixed late this afternoon. Last thing this afternoon — so it's sensible that you get another night here, if you want.'

'Another night. Jolly good. I'll spend it in my bedroom then and let you and the divine Kyle talk cousinly things. Goodnight, Zac. I'll see you tomorrow.' She went to close the door on him, trying not to cry, but he put his hand on it and pushed against it.

'Seriously?' There was an edge to his voice that she hadn't heard for a very long time. Not since she had thrown a tantrum at uni, when her grade hadn't been as good as she had expected. Zac had pointed out that if she spent more time studying and less time in the bars, she might have achieved a higher grade.

Zac had always been bloody annoying like that. He was also, she had yelled at him, boring. But when he got an overall First and she got a 2:1, based on that very assignment, she had to reluctantly agree that he had a point.

She pulled the door open again and looked at the floor. 'Sorry,' she said. Her bottom lip was wobbling treacherously, but she wouldn't let him see her cry. Poor Taigh Fallon, being razed to the ground! And poor Jeanie, putting her trust in her great-nephews for them to do that.

There was an almost imperceptible sigh. 'Do you want to talk about anything?' Zac asked.

'No.' She stepped outside, into the

corridor, and glanced over his shoulder towards the staircase that led up to the tower room. Just one more night here, with the tower room and all the secrets Taigh Fallon had to offer.

She tried to smile and felt it wobble a bit more, but Zac seemed mollified at least. 'I think,' he said, 'that we need to go out tonight. It would do you good to see something outside the house. The mechanic told me there's a ceilidh on in the village. Do you have your dancing shoes with you?'

Angel looked up at him, interested, despite the fact he had arranged to sell Taigh Fallon and she didn't think she'd ever forgive him. But — she quashed the irritation down — it was nothing to do with her, after all.

'A ceilidh would be nice. Can I dance in boots?'

Zac laughed. 'You can dance in whatever you like.'

'Is Kyle coming?'

'Of course. That's not a bad thing, is it?' There was a definite twinkle in his eye. He knew her answer.

She rolled her eyes heavenwards. 'Just tell me when I need to be ready for. I'm intending to hide in a long, deep bubble bath and need to organise my time.'

'Seven o'clock.' Zac grinned. 'The car should be delivered around six. I'll drive. I'll leave you be until then.'

'Hmmm. Does he *have* to come?'

But Zac just laughed and strode away.

★   ★   ★

Kyle was flicking through an old Scottish lifestyle magazine. He had found it on the shelf under the coffee table in the main room with the fireplace in it, and was quite content sitting there in the peace and quiet, the grandfather clock ticking behind him.

He closed his eyes and imagined for a moment living here in its heyday — Laird of the Manor, kind of thing. He wondered if he would have been one of these Scottish, poetical types that roamed the moors composing poetry, or whether he'd have been an older gentleman, wrapped in a tartan blanket, a nightcap on his head, sipping whisky by firelight.

He opened his eyes, a smile playing on his lips. He was maybe more for the moors and the lochs than the nightcap and tartan blanket. He was definitely warming to this cold, dreary land he'd dreaded visiting, just a few days ago. A rustle disturbed him, followed by what he could only describe as a shift in the energy of the room. The scent of heather and waterfalls tickled his nose and his heart began to beat a little faster.

He turned in the seat and saw her standing at the foot of the stairs, smoothing down her dress, looking at the floor, her hair curling over her shoulders. The evening sun streaming through the window cast it with a reddish glow; then she looked up and blotted out the light, so the rays made a halo around her head instead.

For a moment, another face overlaid hers. A younger woman with brighter eyes; then his angel was back, as if she had stepped out of the mirror and into the hallway.

His angel?

Stupid, overactive imagination.

He tossed the magazine to one side and stood up. He searched for a suitably cutting greeting, but found no desire to do that — not right now. Not at this moment.

'Does it look okay?'

He blinked, surprised by the fact she had asked his opinion. The bodice of her gown was closely fitted, plunging black lace on a sheer sort of grey fabric. Tiny beads and crystals studded the lace, and the skirt — three quarter length and a soft, dove grey — was more cobweb than material. The lace from the bodice ran down into five evenly spaced points, just below her hips; and now he studied it more closely, he could see black roses, made out of lace, clustered in the bodice. He never thought he'd ever hear himself say it, but the design went crazily well with the tattoo on her inner wrist.

Her face had a bit more colour as well, with pale pink dusted high on her cheekbones and ruby red lipstick, pulling his gaze to her soft mouth instead of arresting his attention on those dark eyes. He took a step closer to her and the pink on her cheeks deepened. He half-smiled. It wasn't make-up then. That was her, Angel Tempest, blushing.

Maybe she had also found it strange, the fact that she had asked him if she looked okay. It was an interesting thought.

'More than okay,' he heard himself say. 'What made you bring a dress like that to a place like this?'

'You just never know.'

He nodded, taking another step closer to her. He was close enough to inhale that scent. There was an undertone of roses in her perfume. She moved towards him at the same moment and there was that odd, half-remembered crackle in the air between them, the one he'd felt in the corridor and in the tower room. Their eyes fixed on one another and he reached out a hand, just to touch her, just to check she was real . . .

My angel.

God help him, if Zac didn't come in quickly, he'd end up kissing her. His hand was already on her waist; he was pulling her towards him and she wasn't resisting. He leaned down, at the same time as she tilted her face upwards. It was like the workings of a clock — everything fitted, everything was playing out as it should . . .

He tangled his fingers in her curls and bowed down towards her, leaning his head on hers, closing his eyes and pulling her closer.

She did not resist. She clung to him as he picked her up and carried her up the oak staircase —

'Looking good, Miss Tempest!'

They sprang apart as Zac came hurrying down the stairs, tugging at the sleeves of his clean shirt.

'I'm not sure what the locals will make of you,' continued Zac, 'but I think you're perfectly attired.'

Angel spun around and curtsied, exaggeratedly, at him. 'Thank you, good sir. I don't actually give a damn what the locals think. This is me. This is my party dress. They can admire it or they can stare at me. God knows I'm used to it.'

'Not so much at home, though,' said Zac with a grin. 'Kyle.' Zac nodded at Kyle, and Kyle was sure there was a kind of smirk on his cousin's face.

He moved away from Angel, and pushed his hand through his hair. 'Zac. You ready?'

'I am,' he said. 'Shall we go?'

'Oh!' Angel raised a hand. 'No. Sorry. I just have to dash back upstairs. I forgot something. I'll see you outside.'

She melted away into the shadows, a cobweb flitting through the night, and disappeared. She didn't turn back and Kyle knew that the moment was lost.

The harsh reality was that whatever bridge they'd built, it probably couldn't withstand an evening in each other's company.

* ★ ★ ★

Angel hadn't forgotten anything. Of course she hadn't. She just wanted to be away from him.

That almost-kiss at the bottom of the stairs had shaken her. What she *had* almost forgotten, was that she was supposed to hate this man — this man who was going to steal Taigh Fallon from underneath Zac's feet; this man who had been nothing but a sour-faced horror since the moment she had found him creeping up the stairs in the middle of the night.

By rights, she *should* hate him. He was going to block the corridors in. He was going to swindle Zac out of his inheritance. He was going to knock this lovely old property down and build fifty townhouses or something in its place . . .

Well okay, maybe that was a bit of an exaggeration, but she was positive he'd try to develop the land somehow. He wouldn't just buy the house as a holiday home. She hadn't even gone into her room. She was in the little corridor, staring along towards the tower room. She placed her palm on the wall, and wondered how many other people had stood in this very spot, looking along the hallway to the end of the passage, ready to be invited in to that room.

As she stood, she thought she saw the door open and candlelight flicker within. She blinked, and it looked exactly as it had done two minutes ago — closed and darkened. But just to be on the safe side, she hurried along to check there was nothing in the room that might cause a fire. If they were all going out for the evening, the place could burn down quite unnoticed.

When she reached it, the door was shut firmly and the voices were murmuring behind it again. But there was something else. A woman's sob, as if she was in pain or in great distress. Angel flung the door open, and stared into the room. It was lit pleasantly from the evening sun going down in the west, cosy and friendly as always.

She stepped back into the corridor and shut the door firmly.

Then she ran all the way back to the staircase and flew down it, into the human company she knew awaited her there.

1897

He couldn't help but remember it. He was the person who had brought her to this moment. He, Alasdair Fallon . . .

It had been the previous year when they'd been alone in the house. Connor was away on business and Annis never liked being alone. She had begged him to stay the night. He had wavered, indecisive, until the storm came. Thrashing across the Loch, it battered the house until rivulets ran down the windows and hailstones bombarded the cast-iron fireplaces. It was late summer; they hadn't bothered with fires.

With nobody to mitigate it, nobody to prevent it happening, they found themselves embracing. They kissed, a momentary madness, the result of a hunger and a jealousy that had built up for years bursting forth as he nuzzled her neck and she jerked her head back, gasping with pleasure. He loosened her hair and let it fall down to her waist; she undid his shirt with shaking hands as he tangled his fingers in her curls and bowed down towards her, leaning his head on hers, closing his eyes and pulling her closer.

She did not resist. She clung to him as he picked her up and carried her up the oak staircase. The servants did not live in the house — nobody would ever know. He shouldered the door to their bedroom, hers and Connor's, and gently placed her onto the floor before him. He ran his hands down her shoulders, pushing her gown down inch by blessed inch, and a little noise caught in her throat. He leaned down and ran his lips across that throat, rewarded by her groan of ecstasy and the sharp stab of her nails digging into the soft flesh of his biceps.

Then the atmosphere shifted, as if they knew they were racing against time. Their remaining clothes tumbled to the ground as they tore them off one another. He picked her up again and lifted her onto the bed. They joined with the ease of lovers who had known each other forever.

Finally, he arched above her, collapsing onto her with her name on his lips, her hair damp and curling on the pillows.

'Annis, Annis,' he breathed, filling his lungs with her scent. 'What have you done to me?'

'I know not,' she said, her voice unsteady. 'I only know what you have done to me — '

A creak on the stairs, heavy footsteps echoing through the house; a heartbeat as they stared at each other.

'Who is it?' she whispered, clinging onto him. 'Nobody should be here.' Her voice rose in panic as she looked at the door. 'Connor...'

'Sshhhh. It will not be him. He is in London. I had word from him only yesterday.'

'Then who is it?' She struggled to sit up, staring panic-stricken at the door.

'Let me go.' He climbed out of bed, pulling his breeches on quickly. He took a poker from the fireplace and padded across the room.

'Alasdair! Be careful, oh please be careful — '

'Sshhh. Stay there, I won't be harmed, I promise.'

Annis did as she was bid, huddled in the covers, watching the door.

There was a commotion, a shout, a scream; the sound of something falling, falling, hitting the stairs, bouncing down them. A new sound — the sound of a cry, another shout. The clatter of the poker hitting the wooden floor. Angry sobs, protestations.

Annis felt sick. She crawled out of the bed, dragging the sheet behind her, wrapping herself in it; already feeling a choking guilt for what she had done to Connor.

She stepped into the corridor, and walked cautiously towards the staircase. She looked down over the banister; she clamped her hand over her mouth to stifle a scream.

'I did nothing. I swear. I did nothing.'

Alasdair was crouched by the broken body of another man, cradling his head in his lap, tears streaking his face in the moonlight.

'Oh God!' He was rocking backwards and forwards. 'He fell, I swear, he did not expect me to challenge him. He stepped backwards into nothing.'

The dead man was Connor; a great gash in his head, his eyes open and startled, staring at something only he could see.

The images of that night would never leave either of them.

They never knew whether the London letter was delayed in transit, for the dead man had omitted to date it. They never knew whether Connor intended to catch his wife with another lover; whether he had suspicions or not. They never knew whether Connor's return to Taigh Fallon was as innocent as a man simply catching an earlier train to come home to his wife.

They never knew so many things.

Afterwards, Annis had turned to the tower room, to her candles and her mirror and her all-consuming guilt.

And Alasdair wished with all his heart that it had never happened . . . that he had never compromised her in that one moment of madness. But it was too late now.

20

The ceilidh at least took her mind off Angel's immediate problems — those being how she felt about Taigh Fallon, the fact that she was now pretty convinced there was something other-worldly in that tower room and the fact that, as she sat in the back of Zac's 4×4 and stared at the back of Kyle's head, she couldn't help but notice how his dark hair curled over his collar and how the back of his neck was tanned by the Canadian weather.

The people at the ceilidh, on the other hand, were more entranced by Angel's outfit than the fact that she was one third of a trio that were clearly strangers to the village. Once they had realised who the three of them were, Zac, being Zac, soon had most of the single females, of all ages, hovering around him asking questions about

Skye and Taigh Fallon and dear Jeanie and how long did he intend to stay? Kyle seemed to keep people at a cool distance, smiling and engaging with them when he had to, but preferring to stand on the edges, watching.

Angel basked in the compliments, and chatted to the little girl who came up to her to touch her skirts shyly and stare at the stud in her nose. She reminded her of Grace.

'I've never been to one of these before,' Kyle remarked to Angel, his voice interrupting her thoughts as she stood to one side with her glass of red wine. 'Not the sort of thing you get in Ontario.'

Angel looked up at him. Part of her was surprised that he was deigning to speak to her; part of her wasn't. But it was perhaps best to try and communicate on a very general level after the scene on the staircase. And she was trying her best to get over the idea of him buying Zac out for development because it was nothing to do with her.

So, for Zac's sake, fortified by a large gulp of wine, Angel nodded. 'You don't get many in Whitby either. I've been to a couple with Zac on Skye, and they're always good fun. Not that I'm very good at the dancing, though.'

This particular ceilidh was in nothing more glamorous than a church hall but it was a beautiful church hall, nonetheless, with large stained glass windows and polished wooden floors.

'I wouldn't know how to do the dances at all,' said Kyle, watching the people fling themselves around the floor, spinning and laughing, grabbing the hands of their partners as they galloped around in circles or in lines. He almost smiled; well, his lips curved ever so slightly upwards and a couple of crinkles appeared at the corner of his eyes. 'I guess that's why that guy keeps barking out instructions — for novices like me.'

Angel watched as Zac whirled past with a red-haired girl and nodded. 'I need instructions too. It's nothing to be ashamed of.'

'Shall we not be ashamed together then?'

The question was so unexpected that Angel almost choked on her wine. She glugged the rest of the glass down and looked at him. 'Pardon?'

'I'm trying to ask you to dance.' He had that half-smile going again, and the crinkles at the corner of his eyes emphasised the burning gaze he fixed her with.

'Oh. Gosh. Thank you. Yes.' The response was silly and inadequate, but she didn't really know what else to say. 'I'm really not very good.'

'Neither am I.' He held out his hand and she put the empty wine glass on a table, and reached out. Their fingers touched, laced together easily, as if they'd done it before. He bowed, ever so slightly, and led her out to the dance floor.

'Just in time for Strip the Willow!' shouted the caller from the front of the hall. 'Take your places in the line!'

Kyle and Angel, by mutual, silent

agreement, chose the middle of the line. Angel glanced up at Kyle and he raised his eyebrows in mock-despair. She dipped her head so he couldn't see her smile, then turned her attention to the caller.

'And here we go,' cried the man. 'Top couple, take each other's hands . . . '

The dance was more fun with Kyle than Angel would ever have admitted. She found herself laughing at his fumbled steps, whirling around — usually in the wrong direction — and spinning around the other dancers until she was almost dizzy.

They slid into two or three other dances at which they seemed to become less and less proficient, until, during the Lomond Waltz, they suddenly found their rhythm, Angel held firmly in Kyle's arms.

It felt quite nice. She closed her eyes, and found herself moving easily, choreographed perfectly in a dance that seemed to be made for them. All thoughts of him spoiling Taigh Fallon drifted out of her mind, and she was in another place, another time . . .

'*Connor is watching,*' *she said, giggling.* '*See him! Oh Alasdair, see your poor brother.*' *She peeped over his shoulder and smiled at the man standing at the edge of the ballroom. Connor raised his glass at her as she was whisked away, turning circle after circle . . .*

She snapped her eyes open, back in the church hall — or rather she wasn't. She was being waltzed out of the door, into the cooler evening air. There was a little knot garden — some sort of apothecary's garden, she assumed, filled with healing plants in little beds, and the scent of mint and rosemary tickled her nose.

'At last. Fresh air. That was some workout,' Kyle said. He released her and it was a moment before her head stopped spinning to match her body. 'We seem to be the perfect dance partners, if nothing else.'

'Yes. We were well-matched in there.'

She broke off a mint leaf and crumbled it between her fingers, inhaling its scent. 'Neither of us were very good.'

'Until the end.' Amusement coloured his voice. 'Anyway, the reason I brought you out here, was because I don't beat about the bush. We didn't get off to a good start. We don't like each other and we barely tolerate one another. However — ' And before Angel could protest, he grabbed her to him and kissed her. Just as swiftly, he let her go and she stumbled a little, wondering whether she had dreamed it. But no — her lips felt hot and she was breathing in the tang of his aftershave, the scent overlaying the herbs that surrounded her.

He stood back and looked at her, his brows knitted into a frown. 'As I said. However. And I really shouldn't have done that. I'm sorry. You'll *really* hate me now. Both of you.'

'Yes, you *should* be sorry,' she stammered out. Then before she fell into a void she felt she'd never climb out of alive, she checked herself and pointed her forefinger at him. 'This does not change anything,' she said. 'In fact, it just might make things worse.'

'I deserve that,' he murmured, 'I guess I really do.' And he stepped away from her side.

'Hey guys! There you are!' Zac's voice carried through the night air. 'I saw you disappear.'

★   ★   ★

Angel turned, deeply mortified, and just in time to face Zac, who was coming through the thyme-edged pathways towards them. 'Zac!' She called, rather too brightly, and waved her arm in the air. 'You've got the ladies entranced in there. Not bad for a crofter.'

'Ah, we crofters know how to dance, though. Anyway, they're winding up. Someone's started singing the 'Skye Boat Song' and the dancing's been forgotten.'

'Oh I love that song,' cried Angel.

She picked up her skirt and hurried away, between the men. 'Nothing more romantic than the Jacobites,' she threw back over her shoulder.

Indeed, she thought very few things were as romantic as the Jacobites — this song, which celebrated Flora Macdonald helping Bonnie Prince Charlie escape from Skye and the story behind one of her favourite places, Soldier's Leap at Killiecrankie, where a fleeing Redcoat pursued by angry Jacobites had leapt eighteen feet across the River Garry to escape. 'I might catch 'Loch Lomond' if they're finishing up.'

Traditionally, 'Loch Lomond' always ended the ceilidhs Angel had attended with Zac. The sorrowful, beautiful lyrics almost always had her in tears — depending on how much she'd had to drink; especially the second verse, which mourned the loss of the singer's beloved:

As weel may I weep, O yet dreams
  in my sleep,
we stood bride and bridegroom

together,
but his arms and his breath were as
  cold as the earth,
and his heart's blood ran red in the
  heather.

Instead of going back into the hall, though, she ran around to the other side of the building — and out of sight, beneath the big stained glass window, she leaned her hot cheeks against the cool stonework for a moment, then turned and slid down the wall. She sat with her cobwebby skirt bunched up around her and wrapped her arms around her legs. She rested her face on her bent knees, but still her cheeks burned up.

That man! That dratted man! She had to remember she hated him. She had to remember that his intention was to take Taigh Fallon away from Zac and she wouldn't put it past him to be using her to pursue his own ends. If he fussed over her and pretended he found her attractive, she might agree, starry-eyed, to have a chat with Zac about it all.

'No,' she said into her knees, the grey fabric scratchy against her skin where tiny crystals glittered. 'I can't let it happen.'

From behind her, floating out of the window, the last notes of the 'Skye Boat Song' died away and the well-loved chords of 'Loch Lomond' began.

Never had it ever seemed so mournful, and never had she felt so emotional listening to it. By the time the end of the song came, the cobweb stuff of her skirt was drenched with tears. It was a good job, she thought bitterly as she stood up and composed herself, smoothing the fabric down and tugging at the bodice, that her eye make-up was waterproof.

★   ★   ★

Angel always got like that with 'Loch Lomond', Zac thought, glancing at her in the rear-view mirror. She didn't look very cheerful, but she didn't seem very

208

drunk — the amount of alcohol con-
sumed was usually on a sliding scale
along with how maudlin his friend became,
and that's why it seemed out of character tonight.

He was driving them back to Taigh
Fallon and it was colder now, the stars
beginning to prick through the veil of
the night sky. His cousin seemed
preoccupied as well, for some reason.
Zac suspected tonight's sliding scale
was more on a par with how the pair of
them had behaved.

It hadn't escaped his notice that they'd
disappeared from the hall, but it wasn't
until his partner — an extraordinarily
pretty brunette with the figure of a true
dancer — had commented that she'd seen
them head out into the gardens, that he
had known where they had vanished to.
So, to save any potential bloodshed or
Angel slapping his cousin hard for some
imagined misdemeanour, he had made
his excuses to the brunette, and went
after them.

Which is when he'd found Angel

running off, and Kyle glowering in the shadows. Ah well, you couldn't prevent everything could you?

21

'Thanks for driving, Zac. I'm going to make a start packing. We'll be heading home tomorrow, I guess, so it's just easier if I prepare now,' Angel said. They'd pulled up in front of the house and she had slipped out of the car and was hovering by the front door.

'Can't I tempt you into a nightcap?' asked Zac, as he opened the door and waved her inside.

She smiled and shook her head. 'Not tonight, thanks.' Then she disappeared upstairs like a ghost.

'That's not like her,' Zac remarked. 'She's normally up for one. Oh well.' He shook his head. 'You?' he asked Kyle, who shrugged and looked uncomfortable.

'I dunno,' said Kyle. His eyes followed Angel and Zac smiled.

'You could probably do with one. She

has that effect on people.'

'Have you been together long?'

The question was so unexpected, it made Zac spill a little of the whisky he was pouring into his glass. He gestured with the bottle to a second glass and Kyle finally nodded. He looked a bit pale and haunted in the lamplight, and Zac gave him a little extra measure.

'Angel and I aren't together. We're just friends.'

'Friends with benefits? No — sorry, that was out of order.' Kyle took the glass and raised it to Zac. He took a drink and stared into the amber liquid. 'Never sure if you should add water to this or not.'

'Personal taste. I take it neat, Angel likes it with water. And believe me, we don't have benefits like you suggest. Once — and once only, thank God.' He grinned, remembering. 'But no. As far as I know, she's single.'

Kyle glanced at him his brows drawn together. 'You shared a room last night, didn't you?'

'Aye. But she'd just come across a maniac on the stairs.'

'Touché.' Kyle raised his glass and took another sip. 'Did you give my offer any more consideration?'

'Aye! I think it would work. Shall we talk? There's plenty more whisky in the bottle.'

'Talking's great,' replied Kyle. 'I've got all night.'

★　★　★

Angel wasted no time. She packed up everything she could, as quickly as she could. She left one set of clothes out, along with her toiletries, and everything else went in the carpet bag; except her cobweb gown. She left that hanging up from the wardrobe door to let the creases drop out. It was her favourite dress, and she would fold it carefully and lay it on the top of her packing in the morning.

Other than that, she took her make-up off, brushed her hair and slid miserably in between the cool sheets. She stared into the darkness and eventually closed her eyes. Kyle's face floated in front of her and she flipped over angrily, ramming the pillow over her head. It didn't do much to keep her thoughts at bay though.

Tomorrow she'd be back at the croft, then the night after back at home in Whitby. The thought was appealing. After tomorrow, she wouldn't have to see Kyle again. But it was annoying to think she couldn't protect Zac from his cousin's plan. The fact that she knew her time in Taigh Fallon was so limited made her open her eyes again. She stared into the pillow, pulled it off her head and tossed it to one side. She slid back out of bed and went over to the window. It would do no harm to look at Eilean Donan for a little while; sleep was clearly evading her.

As she imagined the castle in its heyday and its history and floating off in a boat with Bonnie Prince Charlie, she heard a swishing sound behind her.

She ignored it, supposing the cobweb dress had slipped off its hanger.

Surely, she reasoned, her gaze roving over the ruins, it wouldn't be out of the question to have a little wander to the tower room tonight. The view would be perfect out of those windows, and she wouldn't even have to try to avoid Kyle as his rooms were on the other side of the house. She moved away from the window and left her room, quietly shutting the door behind her. She walked along the quiet passageway, hearing male voices and the odd, short burst of laughter drift up from downstairs. Zac and Kyle were clearly bonding and who was she to stop them, she thought bitterly. She felt more confused than ever about Kyle and could cheerfully wring Zac's neck for his easy-going stupidity.

Angel went up the little staircase and eventually came to the door of the tower room. She opened it carefully, listening cautiously before she entered for any phantom murmurings that might be going on in there. Tonight, though, the room was silent.

She stepped inside and an odd, comforting feeling wrapped itself around her. This was a place where someone had come a lot — perhaps for the same reasons she did tonight. Perhaps to look out on those ruins and the black, still water of Loch Duich, and to gather their thoughts. She went over to the window and peered out. She smiled to herself, loving the moonlit ruins and the quiet atmosphere of the room.

Idly, she glanced over at the mirror and her heart stuttered as she recalled the man who had stared out at her. She went over to the glass and leaned closely into it. It was misty tonight; some condensation, maybe. She took part of her nightdress in her hand and rubbed at it. The pictures formed in the reflection and she smiled, contented to see the image of the room she loved so much. Then she frowned. Candles were lit, and there were slips of paper on the table. It was showing her that odd image again and she turned, fully expecting the room to be as bare as it had been when she first walked in.

Instead, she saw the candles flickering in the sconces and smelled the melting wax. Overlaying that, was the scent of rosewater and lilies, and the smell of a wood fire, recently lit. A noise behind her, near the windows, made her spin again. A young woman stood there; a bulky, awkward silhouette in an unflattering black gown. The moonlight painted her hair with silver and she turned her head to look at the secret doorway.

Angel choked back a scream, ramming her fist in her mouth. Then the whole scenario just melted away, fading into the night as if it had never been. She didn't hang around any longer. She ran out of the room and back along the corridor, back down the little staircase, her heart pounding. Had she really just seen a ghost? Had that room showed itself to her as it might have been? Or was she just overtired and overemotional?

It wouldn't be the first time. She plumped, for the sake of her sanity and a good night's sleep, for the overtired explanation and blocked the idea of proper ghosts out of her mind. She absolutely refused to think about the devastatingly handsome, dark-eyed man she had seen in the mirror — because if it wasn't Kyle creeping around, then she didn't want to go there at all. She did, however, spare a thought for Goth Cottage and the supposed ghosts there. She'd never technically *seen* any of them — it was more just a feeling she had, especially in The Room. But here — there was definitely something going on.

On the floor below her, a door shut and she heard Zac and Kyle talking again; the unmistakeable Scottish lilt and the rumbling Canadian tones batting back and forth. She hesitated, wondering if she should go down and speak to them, despite Kyle being there. She wondered if she needed human company or a friendly smile from Zac;

whether she would be mocked or believed if she told them what she thought she might have seen.

But she decided against it. She hurried back into her room and locked the door behind her. There might be ghosts here, or there might not be. But there was definitely a Kyle and she wasn't too sure if she was locking the door to keep him out or, psychologically, keep herself in. She pressed her fingertips to her lips. She could still taste him there, still feel the scratchy stubble of his chin against hers.

She sat back on the window seat and stared out into the darkness again. She had a feeling it was going to be a very, very long night. Much later, when she eventually felt tired enough to crawl back into bed, she looked over at the dress, remembering she had heard it fall before she went to the tower room. She intended to hang it back up.

But it was still hanging up, on the wardrobe door, undisturbed.

It was spring; the spring after he'd seen her wading in the Loch, up to her knees, her skirts held high.

They'd been invited to a dance — it wasn't a ceilidh; it was much more formal. One of the well-heeled families in the area, showing off their wealth and influence. Alasdair didn't have a lot of time or respect for them. Annis and Connor, however, trying to fit into the new money of those influential families, were determined to make a good impression.

Connor had sat out this particular dance, pleading shortness of breath, related to his long-standing heart complaint — residue of his childhood illness. He had passed Annis into Alasdair's care and sat watching them as they whirled past. Alasdair held Annis as if she belonged in his arms, moving easily, choreographed perfectly in a dance that seemed to be made for them.

'Connor is watching,' she said, giggling. 'See him! Oh Alasdair, see your poor brother.' She peeped over his shoulder and smiled at the man standing at the edge of the ballroom. Connor raised his glass at her as she was whisked away, turning circle after circle.

'I hope I have not offended him by dancing with you,' he teased, smiling down at her. But her heart was with Connor. Not him. And Annis was quite the most beautiful girl he had ever seen.

'You could not offend anyone!' she replied, laughing up at him. 'Surely, if my husband is forced to abandon me to any man, then you would be my one and only choice.'

'And if Connor was not here? If you had to choose another man in his place,' he asked, his eyes burning into hers, 'would that man be me? Or am I simply a very poor substitute?' He knew he had had too much to drink, and it made him reckless. But sometimes, he fancied that she felt the same way as he did, although God knows he had tried to hide it. He loved his brother. But he thought he might love Annis as well . . .

'You are not a poor substitute — not at all.' They whirled around and broke away from the dancers. Alasdair whirled her out of the doors, onto the terrace, and brought her to a halt on the stone balcony which overlooked the rock garden below.

Laughing, she pulled away and leaned on the stone balustrades, breathing in the deliciously-scented night air. 'And what are we doing out here, Alasdair Fallon?'

'I need fresh air.' He leaned on the balustrade, his back to the garden, his attention on Annis. 'I wanted to be out here, with you.'

'Aye,' she replied, forgetting her status as a well-connected, well-bred lady. She was, for a moment, the lassie from the glens, revelling in the evening air. 'There is nothing better. Nothing better at all.'

'Do you ever regret the choices you made in your life?' Alasdair asked, pretending nonchalance.

'Choices?' Annis turned and looked up at him. 'What choices?'

Alasdair opened his mouth. He was desperate to reply: your marriage, your choice of husband, your life with him. Instead, he shrugged. 'Moving away from the glens. This, surely, is a mighty city compared with what you left behind.'

Annis smiled. 'It is not really a mighty city! It is not Edinburgh or Inverness or Aberdeen. But yes.' She moved towards him and laid her hand on his chest. 'Sometimes, much of the time, in fact, I wonder if I made the right choice.' She looked into his eyes and he felt himself falling. It was there again, that undercurrent.

He had not been mistaken, and the champagne made him brave. 'I also wonder if you made the right choice,' he replied in a low voice.

'Will we ever know?' she asked, her

voice a whisper, her eyes never leaving his.

He wanted to respond in kind. He wanted to tell her no: she had made the wrong choice, that they had to unravel her choices and make things right. But he also knew it was futile.

'Ah, there you are!' Connor had found them, as always. It was only to be expected.

'Connor! Are you feeling stronger?' Annis moved her attention smoothly to her husband. Perhaps only Alasdair noticed the falsely ingratiating edge to her voice.

'Yes thank you.' Connor moved slickly in between them, and Alasdair fought back a rage which burned him from within.

'We were too hot in there.' Annis moved into her husband's arms for an embrace. 'It's much cooler out here. I'm glad you thought to join us.'

'I too am pleased I joined you,' replied Connor. 'My wife and my brother. What could be better?' He glanced sideways at Alasdair, then effectively dismissed him by looking away; although, being Connor Fallon, he did it with a smile and a formal inclination of his head.

Alasdair nodded and tugged his jacket straighter. He knew when he was defeated.

22

Finally, the dawn crept up on her. Fresh, golden light sent tendrils through the window, the early morning sun splitting the trees.

Angel turned over and stared blearily at the carpet bag. In an instant, she remembered its purpose and her heart sank. Just her few toiletries and her cobweb dress to go in, then she'd be packed. Uncomfortably, she remembered the swishing noise she'd heard last night and dragged her gaze over to the dress. It must have been her imagination — the sheets sliding off the bed or the curtains blowing in the breeze.

She pushed the covers back and sat on the edge of the bed, wiggling her bare toes. There was nothing for it — she had to get up and, ugh, probably face Kyle over her toast. She slipped off the bed and tugged the sheets straight over the warm patch she'd been snuggled in. Another sigh as she realised it would probably be the last time she woke up to this view and slept in this bed. She trailed into the en-suite and showered, memorising every last angle of every last item in the bathroom, then wandered back out, twisting her long hair into a towel as she folded up her cobweb dress and shook out her clothing for today; a long, fairly plain, black dress with a nipped in waist and a deep sweetheart neckline, and the boots she had worn last night to the ceilidh. A slick of lip gloss and a couple of coats of mascara, a thick line of kohl around her eyes and her hair loose, and that was it.

She clicked the bag shut and made sure everything was tidy in the room, then hauled her belongings downstairs, where she left the carpet bag and her handbag in the middle of the main room.

'I thought that was you.' Zac appeared, cradling a cup of coffee. 'Come on, have some breakfast. I'll get those for you later. I take it you're coming back with me today?'

Angel nodded. 'It's been lovely. I adore this house, I really do. The ceilidh was amazing and being here, with Eilean Donan over the Loch is just awesome. It's so close — just over the water. And I've enjoyed spending time with *you*.' She pasted a smile on her face and punched him heartily on the shoulder. 'Just me and you.'

'And Kyle,' he said with a smirk. 'I bet *you've* enjoyed meeting Kyle.' He punched her, equally heartily back, earning himself the blackest scowl that Angel could dredge up at that moment.

'I have *not* enjoyed meeting Kyle.'

Zac grinned. 'Whatever. Look, I have to go to the solicitor this morning. It shouldn't take too long, so I'll head there first thing and come back for you. Is that okay?'

Angel nodded.

She pointed to the kitchen. 'Is he in there?'

'No. He's gone for a walk.'

'Then I'll have breakfast in peace,' she responded and linked his arm. 'Escort me, Mr Fallon, please.'

'As you wish, Miss Tempest,' he replied with the smallest of bows. And gracefully, they promenaded through Taigh Fallon, Angel's immediate thoughts on a hot cup of coffee.

'He's not going to pop up through the ice house corridor, is he?' mused Angel, wondering if her nemesis would leap out of the door just to annoy her.

Zac shook his head. 'No. We had a look last night after you'd gone to bed. The floor's unsafe. Kyle said he knew someone who could fix it, and he's going to get in touch with him.'

'What's the point of that? It's not going to benefit anyone, is it?'

'Well maybe not me,' consented Zac.

'He's just looking to rip the place up from the inside out. I wouldn't trust him.'

'He seems to know what he's doing. And he seems to be very good at it.'

'Don't let him near your property,

Zac,' begged Angel. 'He's a bad-tempered, self-serving horror.'

'A horror who knows what he's doing with property and land!' replied Zac, laughing at her description.

'But what about Jeanie?'

'What about her?'

'She left this place to *you*.'

'No. She left it to us *jointly*. And I don't want it.'

Angel knew when she was beaten. She reminded herself it was nothing to do with her — nothing at all. 'Fine. Whatever you want to do then. Just do it.'

1897

The birth was prolonged and dangerously so. Several times, the midwife and the doctor thought she was slipping away. The baby was coming early and they worried it would affect her more than was usual.

He waited outside the room, powerless to help. He sat, his back to the wall, staring at the staircase without properly seeing it, trying not to hear the screams beyond the door. At some point, he sought a pencil and some paper. He took up his position again and began to sketch; just as he had done when he was a child and wanted to escape the world around him. Just as he had done when his brother had lain so ill and his father had been supervising the building of Taigh Fallon as well as dealing with his wife's hysterics over the boy's future. When Connor had married, the house had become his wedding gift.

The lines drew themselves, his conscious mind unaware of what he was producing. When he finally focused on the paper, he saw her. He saw the face of his angel — her eyes hypnotising him from the paper, the strange markings on her wrist wreathing the edges of the page.

'Let all be well, my angel, let all be well,' he repeated. 'Let them both survive the birth.'

They did. A son was delivered in the

twilight of the third day; a child who bore the Fallon eyes and the Fallon colouring. Annis, feverish and exhausted, repeated to all who would listen how he resembled his dead father. Alasdair hovered in the shadows, seeing in the babe his own eyes, the shape of his own chin, the colour of his own hair.

He sat by the side of the bed, stroking her hair back from her face when they were alone. This is what it would be like, he told himself, if she had ever been truly mine.

He wished he could claim them both, but knew it was impossible. The guilt over his brother gnawed away at him; even more so as he watched Annis change hourly.

The madness crept upon her so slowly as to be almost indistinguishable from the exhaustion and elation that she see-sawed between.

She spoke of her dead husband as if he was still alive; held conversations with him, responding as him, as he would in life. She dismissed the nursemaid, hysterical, accusing the woman of wanting to steal her child. *She would not listen to reason. She refused to see anyone but Alasdair. She turned her face away from doctors and refused to speak.*

Soon, she and Alasdair were the only people in the house apart from the invisible staff who kept a safe distance from the mistress.

'I must go to him,' she said on the morning of the fourth day. 'He is waiting for me by the Loch. He says he will meet me at Eilean Donan. I have always loved it there. It is not too far, is it, my love?' *She turned her pale face towards him, seeking his approval.* 'It's just over the water.' *She knew at least it was he, Alasdair, who sat with her, at that time; not Connor.*

'Not too far at all, my love,' he said.

She nodded. 'I thought not.' *She pulled herself into a sitting position.*

He placed his hand gently on her shoulder. 'Perhaps when you are stronger, Annis.'

She lay back on the pillows and

233

nodded again. 'It won't be long. Tell him I will meet him there, will you?'

'I will tell him,' he said. She closed her eyes and he stroked her forehead until she slept.

He waited for a while, watching her, then left her to rest.

23

After Zac had left, still defending Kyle and his property development, Angel knew she had to visit that tower room one last time. There was a pull towards it. Maybe it was the fact the windows let in more light and more of the Highlands than any other room. When she leaned into the leaded panes, she was high over the tree tops and felt as if she could almost reach out and skim her hands over the branches.

Or maybe it was the mirror that greeted her silently every time she went in. Now, she stood in front of it, looking intently for the face of the man who had flickered there on and off for the last couple of days. He wasn't there — it was just a reflection of the empty room behind her — with no sign, even, of the room it had showed her from so many years ago. This morning, in the daylight, she thought it might have been more of a dream than a reality — more a case of her imagination putting things together. She was a highly creative person after all. Nobody ever said her mind was logical.

There was a noise behind the bookshelf though — somewhere on the spiral staircase, or beyond that, in the corridor even. Angel went over to the concealed entrance and put her ear against the wood. There it was again — it was like a cat mewing or crying . . . In fact —

'It's a baby!' Angel had heard enough babies squalling in her workshop to recognise the sound of a newborn in distress. 'How on earth . . . ?' She looked around. There must be a switch or a latch somewhere that opened the thing. She felt all around the edge of the door and when that failed, she moved onto the bookshelf, reaching up as high as she possibly could. Her fingers closed over something and she grabbed it, jumping back as the bookcase sprung open.

She poked her head inside the little room; the noise was louder, and there was singing — a faint tune she recognised from her trips to Skye: 'The Braes of Balquhither', a beautiful old folk song from the early 1800s. Many people knew some of the refrain from the modern song 'Wild Mountain Thyme', but as she listened, she understood this to be the original version.

> *I will twine thee a bower,*
> *By the clear siller fountain,*
> *And I'll cover it o'er*
> *Wi' the flowers o' the mountain;*

'Who's there?' Angel shouted. 'What are you doing?'

The breathy, haunting melody continued:

> *I will range through the wilds,*
> *And the deep glens sae dreary,*
> *And return wi' their spoils*
> *To the bower o' my deary.*

'Look, you shouldn't be here,' Angel shouted again. But at the same time, icy little fingers of fear prickled the skin between her shoulder blades. Logic told her it was impossible for a woman and a child to be down there. This door was locked — the shore was private property. Unless she'd swept in on a boat, broken into the well-concealed ice house door or snuck in through the entrance from the kitchens, nobody could have been there.

Angel leaned into the doorway a bit further. 'Hello?'

> Now the summer is in prime,
> Wi' the flowers richly blooming,
> And the wild mountain thyme
> A' the moorlands perfuming;

A wail from the baby, who was clearly more distressed now than before, matched with a *shush*-ing noise from the woman. There was a brief silence and Angel stepped fully into the room, then the cry started up again. It really did seem as if there were a couple of people down there.

> To our dear native scenes
> Let us journey together,
> Where glad innocence reigns
> 'Mang the braes o' Balquhither.

Angel's mind played over a few different scenarios: travellers, runaways, a young girl seeking help and shelter? Squatters, even?

'No,' she said firmly, out loud. 'There can't be anyone. Hello? *Hello*!'

The singing died away and there was the sound of footsteps hurrying away down the stairs and disappearing into the corridors. Angel forced herself to swallow her fear and go after the woman. She remembered a policeman once telling her that if you wanted to apprehend a criminal and they had a child with them, you should go for the child. Natural instinct would be to stay with the child and not run away. This, she determined, would be what she did — although to be fair the only child she'd had much to do with was Grace Nelson.

She wiped sweaty hands on her skirt and shouted once more. 'Okay, you've had fair warning. I'm coming down so you'd better have a decent explanation.'

It was only as she stepped fully into the room and got halfway down the stairs, following that phantom crying, that she heard the heavy bookcase swing back into place and thud, dully, at the top of the stairs.

'Oh great. Oh bloody great,' she shouted. 'You'd better have that bottom door open so we can get out of here!' She grabbed hold of the handrail and ran as fast as she dared down the old stone staircase, now she'd effectively been plunged into darkness. She reached the bottom and flung the door open into the corridor, so at least she got some brackish light coming in from the sky-lights. The crying seemed to be continuing; but not in front of her; behind her. Above her. All around her — echoing, pitiful.

Angel put her hands over her ears and stared around. It was darker down there than she remembered and all together more dreary. Then, it all fell silent. Something swept past her, the brush of a gown against the brick walls, the scent of rosewater and lilies. She shivered and all the hairs on her arms stood up on end.

It was suddenly cold down there — freezing cold — and she wrapped her arms around her body. 'Hello?' She tried again, her breath coming out in little visible puffs, smoky in the semi-darkness. There were more footsteps behind her, thundering through the corridor, a man's heavy breathing accompanying them.

Annis. Annis.

Instinctively, Angel pressed herself against the wall as a black shadow tumbled through the corridor. It resolved itself into the silhouette of a man somewhere up ahead and blotted out the shape of the door. It hovered there and seemed to turn to face her.

Angel!

Her name was spoken wonderingly, then the shadow turned.

Wait for me, my angel. Wait for me. Please. I must —

The door to the ice house flung open and slammed back against the wall. The shadow tumbled out and dissolved, the Loch appearing behind it, bright and sparkling in the sunshine. Angel's legs gave way and she sank to the floor, shaking.

She curled up into the smallest ball she could, and squeezed her eyes shut. A vision flashed into her mind of something white and billowing, tossed on the gentle waves of the Loch. The motion of the water slowly rolled it over and she saw red hair flowing out behind the object; a pale arm, flung out, gracefully like a dancer's as the white thing bobbed and pirouetted in the water.

It was a woman. A dead woman.

Angel opened her eyes quickly, feeling sick to her stomach. The door to the ice house remained open and she stared at it, trying to make sense of what she had seen. The outline of a man filled the doorway again. The man paused, then strode purposefully through the corridor towards Angel. She uncurled herself and stood up, trying to summon up the strength to run or scream or shout. She had no idea, she realised, how to fend off a shadow.

'Angel! Is that you? For God's sake!'

It was with a mingled sense of relief and a sudden anger that Angel recognised the voice as Kyle's.

1897

He was downstairs, pacing, when he was summoned later by the screaming of the baby. It went on and on and on, hysterical.

The housekeeper appeared from the servants' doorway and stared at him, awaiting instructions. Alasdair met her eyes and saw the fear in his own reflected there.

'Annis!' He raced up the stairs two at

a time, the housekeeper following him, all protocol gone as they fled to Annis's room.

He burst in first; the child lay on the floor, too close to the fire she had insisted on. Little Connor's face was scarlet, his limbs flailing within a blanket. One spark, touching that soft, crocheted wrapping and the child would have been burned alive.

'Oh my poor bairn!' The housekeeper swooped down upon him and rescued him, hugging him to her and moving to the window where she wrenched the sash open to let some air in to cool the baby down.

'Annis?' Alasdair stood in the room, the bed unmade, sheets spilling onto the floor where she had slipped away. 'For God's sake! Where are you?' He paused only for a second, before he dashed back out of the room.

He had to trust his instincts. He headed along the corridor and ran up the stairs into the tower room. The door was swinging open. He burst through it, ready to grab her away from the séance she had surely set up. Yet the room was empty. The bookcase, however, was ajar; the doorway to the secret entrance.

'Good God.' He rived the bookcase door further open, calling her name. His voice echoed around the wooden panelled room. The maid's lavender polish had not been used in here for months and the place smelled unaired and unused. 'Annis!' The only sound which answered him was silence.

He raced down the stairs, calling her name. He burst through the tiny hallway; the one she had insisted was fashioned into a small entrance hall, welcoming anyone who dared to use the corridor. He ran past the blue and white vase in the alcove, beneath the mirror she had hung over the doorway, past the comfortable chair that sat, solid, in the corner should anyone ever want to hide away and enjoy some peace and quiet.

He hoped he would find her in the corridor. Images of her stuck in there, shouting for help, banging on the door crowded into his mind. What the hell was she doing anyway?

He is waiting for me by the Loch. He says he will meet me at Eilean Donan.

'Surely not — ' he cried out as the words formed in his mind. 'Not Eilean Donan!'

The thought spurred him on, along the precipitous pathway which led alongside the pit. 'Annis! Annis!'

The place was damp and freezing cold, a huge block of ice in the pit in preparation for the summer — and then he saw her. He saw his angel, standing before him in the corridor. The light coming through the skylights gave her hair a silvery halo and her skin glowed softly pale.

'Angel!' He checked himself. 'Wait for me, my angel. Wait for me. Please. I must — '

And it was when he turned away from her and saw the door opened wide onto the shore of Loch Duich that he knew it. He sprinted towards it and burst out onto the pebbled shore.

It's not far, she had said. It's not far.

Images of her paddling at the shore two years ago, newlywed and laughing came back to him. He and Connor, perched on a fallen tree, watching her.

'Is she not beautiful?' Connor had asked, pouring another dram of whisky into a crystal tumbler for his younger brother.

'Very beautiful,' Alasdair had told him. His gaze followed her slim figure, her ankles peeping out from beneath her dress as she picked her way across the smooth stones. Her auburn hair was coming loose from its pins, blowing in the breeze that trailed across the Loch, leaving endless ripples in its wake.

'It's so cold!' she had cried, laughing towards them. 'Come — come and see. You can tell for yourself.'

'No, thank you!' Alasdair had shouted, smiling, even though it was the very thing he wanted to do, because that way he would be close to her. He had been young and arrogant, and still resented his brother very much for marrying this beautiful lassie from the glens, and wanted to hurt him somehow for doing it: for finding her first.

'You'll catch your death!' Connor had called. 'Come out now.'

She had stopped, holding her dress up, and looked at them. Laughing she shook her head. 'No I won't. Neither will I catch my death, nor will I come out of the water; despite the fact — ' she looked down and lifted one foot out of the water; crystal drops cascaded from her toes, which had taken on a translucent blue-ish sheen ' — that I can no longer feel my extremities.'

Alasdair had laughed, the whisky breaking down the barrier he had carefully constructed over the months of his brother's courtship and marriage. Annis glanced at him and for a moment their eyes met. Something changed and when he smiled again, he knew she reciprocated those feelings. For one moment, it was simply Alasdair and Annis at the Loch. Not Connor. Never Connor.

Annis was the first to look away. She brought her attention back to her feet and paddled around in a little circle, exaggeratedly stomping so the water splashed up and dampened her hem. Alasdair knew it was to hide her blushes.

So, he considered later, did Connor. Alasdair felt a guard go up at that moment between him and his brother.

'I'm a lucky man,' his brother had said, quietly, 'to have married Annis. To have made her my wife. So very lucky.'

It was Alasdair's turn to feel the fire in his cheeks. His brother was happy. And didn't he deserve that chance at happiness? How could he wish it otherwise? He had looked down at the tumbler of whisky in his hand, and the taste of it was sour in his mouth.

Today, as Alasdair stood on the shore searching every corner for her, that carefree time seemed a world away.

'Annis!' He called again. 'Annis! Come back. Your baby needs his mother.' Silence greeted him. He tried a different tactic. 'Connor needs you!' he cried. The words were whipped away by the wind that rushed in from the Loch and he shivered. 'Your child, Connor, is waiting for you!' He hoped the name of the baby would alert her, bring her into his sight. It was no coincidence that he thought the name would remind her of her husband as well.

Still there was no answering call, no rustling as she emerged from the greenery by the side of the shore. He turned and looked up towards the formal gardens, wondering whether she had simply gone back to the house. A black figure came hurrying down the pathway, clutching a small, white bundle: Mrs Rooks, the housekeeper, with the baby.

'Is she there, sir? Is she there?' Mrs Rooks was hugging the child tightly. He had rammed a small fist in his mouth and was asleep, the peril of the fire long forgotten.

'No, I can't see her.' He heard the panic in his own voice. 'She came out by the ice house but I don't know where she went after that — '

His words were interrupted by a piercing screech from Mrs Rooks.

She flung one hand out and pointed to the Loch. 'Dear God! Dear God on high!' She fell to her knees and commenced rocking back and forth, wailing, still pointing and clutching the baby ever closer with her free hand.

Alasdair spun around and saw what that good lady had seen. A white shape in the Loch, floating into view. Facedown, her arms were outstretched, her nightgown billowing up around her as the waves rocked her gently. Auburn hair floated around her, the long curls tangling up around each other.

'Annis!' With no thought for himself, he ran towards the Loch and waded out until he could dive into the water and swim out to reach her. He was a strong, sure swimmer and struck out against the current, not heeding the icy water dragging him down or his shirt clinging to his body.

He grabbed her under the arms and turned her over — he could tell he was too late. Her eyes were half-open and her jaw slack. Her skin was grey; the only colour left to her was her glorious hair even now it was darkened from the water.

It's not too far away, she had said. Just over the water. He knew without a doubt she had plunged into that Loch to reach Eilean Donan; the place where, in her mind, her husband would be waiting for her.

'Annis,' he murmured. He drew her close to him in the water: one final embrace, one more time. 'I'm so sorry.'

The words were inadequate. Even over the keening of the housekeeper, even over the relentless shush of the waves and the fractured thoughts of his dark angel, he was only truly aware of one thing. He numbly brought his brother's wife into the shore and gathered her up to carry her home, one thought marching through his head.

It was all his fault.

24

'How many times do I have to bloody well come in here and haul *you* out of this freakin' corridor?' Kyle was fierce — fiercer than she had seen him before; fiercer, even, than he had been the night she encountered him on the grand staircase.

Angel found her voice and yelled right back at him. 'Nobody asked you to come in and you certainly don't need to haul me out of *anywhere!*' Her hands were curled into fists and, possibly against her better judgement, she began to stomp towards him. He checked himself, his eyes jet-black in the shadows. He looked more like that man from the tower room mirror than ever, all sharp edges and hollow valleys.

'So you're telling me that you're perfectly safe down here? That the floor isn't about to collapse? That another door isn't going to fall down? That the handrail around this damned pit isn't going to crumble away? Tell me — did you even think about letting me know you were in here?'

'I don't need to report to you about *anything*! You're nobody to me — you don't even like me that much, you've just about said that. I should think you'd be pleased if I did die down here. Then you'd be able to manipulate Zac all you liked.' The words were out before she could stop herself.

'Manipulate Zac? What the hell would I want to manipulate him for?'

'For this place!' Angel's voice bounced around the old stonework. 'You know he doesn't want it — and you're just selfish.'

'Selfish?' Kyle laughed, without humour. 'I tell you, I'd be doing him a favour if I took this place off him. It would stop you coming here for a start. Stop you skulking around corridors and killing yourself. In fact, do you know what I'd do?' He came up to her, very close, and pierced her with his eyes. 'I'd have the door sealed shut. Both doors. The door from up *there* — ' he jabbed his forefinger in the direction of the spiral staircase, ' — and the door from over *there*.' This time he pointed behind him to the ice house door. 'And I'd have the tower room blocked off so you couldn't go hide in there.'

'How dare you?' Angel cried. 'You can't do that — stop it!'

'Why? Why did you do it? Why did you come in here? If I hadn't come through here I wouldn't have seen you and I — ' He stopped and stood up straight. He stepped away from her, his expression fathomless, his eyes blank. His voice cracked, pathetically. 'Angel. Why didn't you wait?'

Angel's flesh crawled. It was a weird echo of the words she had heard when the shadow rushed past her, when the man appeared and spoke to her. She began to shake again, staring at Kyle.

She took a deep breath and whispered. 'I saw you. I saw you before, didn't I? Who are you?'

The door behind the man swung open again and she jumped. Behind him in the doorway was the vista of the Loch that she had come to know and love over the last few days; but it was oddly blank and flat — almost like a reflection. Floating, tossed by the waves, was a white figure, trailing auburn hair behind it. Another shape was in the water; darker, stronger, striking out — heading towards the woman.

Angel squeezed her eyes shut and opened them. The flat image had gone. There was just a slice of a rather dull, Highland day and a grey, rain-spotted Loch in view, as the morning's promise of spring sunshine disappeared in rolling clouds coming in from the west. She glanced up at Kyle, whose colour had gradually returned and realised he was staring down at her with that old expression of annoyance and despair.

'You were lucky that door was open,' he growled. She understood, then, that he was back. It was as if that other person had vanished — running through the corridor on some endless, guilt-fuelled trip to see the same horror time after time. Only this time, someone had been there to witness it; to catch it all.

'Did *you* open the door?' She was unable to frame the questions she really wanted to ask.

'No I did not. It was open. I saw someone messing around by the water so I came down to look. It must have been you.'

'Just stop it. Stop it now. Stop bloody accusing me of everything. I've been in here all the time. I came in from the tower room as you so rightly put it.' She was sarcastic and she knew it. 'Because you're always bloody *right*, aren't you?'

She was the one with her face inches from his now. This man was so different to Zac — so different to the cheerful, laid-back friend she had come to view almost as a brother.

'You and Zac would never have made it as a couple,' Rosa had said to her ages ago; sensible, as always. 'He's far too nice for you. You'd get bored too quickly. You need a challenge.'

Angel had laughed at her — but now, now she wondered if it was true.

'Kyle,' she started.

'Shut up.' It was a replay of the ceilidh. He grabbed her and it almost seemed as if he was about to kiss her roughly, but then let her go as if she'd burned him. 'Get out of the corridors!' he said hoarsely. 'It's not safe. How many times do I have to tell you?'

'Don't worry.' She wrenched herself away from him. Tears burned behind her eyes for some stupid reason probably best known to her hormones. 'You'll never have to tell me again, because I'm going now and you know what? I'll never have to see you again either. So that's what I think they call a win-win. I hope you're happy with whatever you do to this place, and I hope you can live with yourself afterwards.'

She pushed past him and ran towards the doorway, bursting out onto the shore and running through the gardens. She thought she heard that singing again; she thought she heard the baby crying. But she simply put her head down and continued to run.

She didn't even bother going back into her room. She just wanted to leave this place and forget she'd ever met Kyle Fallon.

She raced into the big main room, grabbed her handbag from the sofa and ran outside. She would send a message to Zac and have him bring her luggage back. She wasn't waiting for him to finish his trip to the solicitors. She wasn't staying in there a moment longer.

She flew down the long driveway and out of the gates, and turned left towards the village. There was a train station — she remembered passing that. If she got there, she could find her way back to Skye and she'd never have to see him again.

1897

Everyone's thoughts were, of course, for the baby. Tiny Connor Fallon, orphaned before he was a week old. His father dead in a tragic accident, his mother apparently driven to suicide. Theories abounded that the madness had driven her to it; she had undoubtedly suffered from childbed fever and it had affected her mind, burning all sense out of her. God alone knew where she had got the strength to find her way to the Loch though.

Alasdair didn't know much about childbed fever and claimed to know even less about the motives which had driven the young mother to drown herself — although he thought he quite probably understood more than most. The one thing he did assert authority over, was that Connor was to become his ward. He felt responsible for not saving Annis, but the doctors had confirmed she would have been dead within days anyway.

No matter. Little Connor would grow up as his own boy. He would enjoy all the privileges and opportunities he would have had if his parents had survived. The Fallons were a wealthy family — and as it happened, all that wealth had landed upon Alasdair's shoulders, thanks to a convoluted will anticipating that his brother Connor would have no children to pass it on to.

They all said it was a terrible shame. All that doubt, and Connor had fathered a boy after all.

'Just look at him,' they said. 'He's the image of his father.'

And as the boy grew, Alasdair had to agree. He had his father's eyes, no doubt about it.

The Fallons always had dark eyes — every boy in the family had them. Baby Connor was indeed the image of his father.

And Alasdair Fallon loved that child, they all said, as if little Connor was his own son.

25

Kyle stood in the little room at the bottom of the stairs. He had found himself in the tower room and, without thinking, opened the secret door. He had walked down the stairs, almost on auto-pilot, and half-wondered how he had arrived in that small space.

She had gone — long gone. He could tell. The house was just empty. Devoid of energy. After the argument, he had spent two hours stomping around the Loch, clambering over the rocks and onto the path that led around the water, where he had managed to walk most of his temper off.

His mind was whirling — for a moment, it had seemed as if there were more souls in that little room than just the two of them. It had seemed as if it wasn't him and Angel arguing, but other people; people with unfinished business.

Have the door sealed shut. Have the room blocked off. You can't do this — stop it! Why? Why did you do it?

He could barely recall the words he said now — pieces came floating back to him and made him cringe, but he couldn't have told anyone exactly what words were exchanged in there. His mind was simply occupied by her heart-shaped face and her dark eyes. Regardless, they had both been in there, trying to thrash out a whole load of crazy. God, she had been so close to him!

The heat rose again and with it, his temper and his frustration.

Go after her. Go after her.

The voice was a whisper, but it filled the room, nonetheless.

Only one answer remained for that one: 'The Hell I will!' he shouted. 'I've never met a more annoying woman!'

Almost as if he wasn't in control of his movements, he lashed out and grabbed the old vase from the alcove. He picked it up and hurled it against the corner of the arched doorway. It only made him feel better for a very short moment as the china shattered and splintered into fragments.

Then two things caught his attention almost simultaneously: the shadows in the mirror above the doorway that looked, for a brief moment, like two people — a man and a woman, flickering into life then merging together; and the items that were, even now, scattered on the floor amongst the fragments of the vase.

★   ★   ★

Angel made her way to Skye after a train journey to Mallaig that was uncomfortable and annoying, and not without a small amount of second-guessing herself, followed by the ferry over to the island itself.

Why had she even let him get to her? Fair enough, he had more right to be at Taigh Fallon than she did, but did that give him the right to throw his weight around? Demanding the corridor should be shut up and she shouldn't be wandering around it?

As drizzle blew in from the west and spattered Angel with raindrops that dusted her hair with diamonds, she huddled on the deck of the boat and seethed about Kyle.

She got a taxi up from Armadale, hoping that Ivy was still around to at least let her into the studio or the tea room — otherwise she'd be spending the night in her car, waiting for Zac to turn up at whatever time he made it. Fortunately, the girl was as good as her word and despite the fact there was only ten minutes or so to the official closing time, she was still there, running a cloth around the tables and collecting up the last few pieces of discarded crockery.

'Angel!' Ivy looked stunned to see her, and, fair enough, it probably wasn't Angel's best moment. Drenched with the persistent drizzle, her hair sticking to her head, her make-up running and a scowl that would terrify the Devil himself, she must have made a shocking entrance.

'Ivy. I don't suppose Zac is back, is he?' asked Angel. She knew the answer, of course but couldn't think of a conversation opener beyond 'I hate Kyle Fallon and I've run away from Taigh Fallon.'

'Ummm . . . no. Should he be?'

Angel shook her head helplessly, then exploded: 'Oh sod it. I'll be honest. I hate Kyle Fallon and I've run away from Taigh Fallon. I know Zac isn't back. My phone is switched off because I didn't want the hassle, so I'll switch it back on and see how many missed calls I have.'

'Okay.' Ivy looked dazed. 'There's enough coffee left in the percolator if you want one. You look like you could use some caffeine.'

'Thank you. That would be lovely.' Angel threw herself into the closest seat and switched her phone on. She had, in fact, texted him en route and told him she'd be heading to Skye and he needn't wait for her as long as he brought her luggage with him; so as expected, Zac had been messaging her and calling her, trying to find out exactly why she left.

Reluctantly, Angel dialled his number and he answered almost instantaneously. He must have had the thing on speakerphone as there was an odd echo to his words and the soft rumble of an engine in the background.

'Oh *now* you surface!' he moaned at her. 'And where on earth are you?'

'In your tea room,' she responded. 'Drinking your coffee which Ivy very kindly offered me.'

'Are you going to explain what happened?'

'No. Not really. Just let it be known that if I ever see your cousin again, I won't be liable for my actions.'

'He made a good impression then.' Zac's voice was wry.

'He has the worst attitude ever. I can't believe you sprang from the same family tree.'

'Why? Why the bad attitude? What did he do?'

'Oh, he was just ranting about the corridor and how I shouldn't be there and how it was dangerous.'

'Is that all? I would have thought that was being kind and thoughtful.'

Angel paused. 'It didn't seem like him being kind. Anyway. When will you be back?'

'An hour or so?' Zac suggested. 'Just make yourself comfy. Ivy should have a spare set of keys.'

'Thanks. Do you want to speak to Ivy?' Angel looked up at Ivy and smiled as she sat down opposite with a cup of tea.

'No, it's okay. I'll see her tomorrow. She'll have gone home by the time I get back anyway. I can catch up in the morning. Just tell her thank you for holding the fort. Look, I'm losing the signal so I'll go. See you soon.' And with that, he disconnected the call.

Angel looked at the mobile and tossed it onto the table with a sigh; then a gut-wrenching, toe-curling thought struck her as she recalled the obvious pitfalls and potential horror of a speakerphone in the car: 'You know — I *really* hope Zac wasn't giving that man a lift . . . '

★   ★   ★

By the time Zac returned and let himself in, Angel had apparently soaked in a hot bath and was curled up in the sun-room at the back of the croft, flicking through a fashion magazine. Her hair was damp and plaited loosely, and she was wearing a black satin wrap over her nightgown.

'Good evening. It seems as if gemstone jewellery is as popular as ever,' she said. 'I'm not surprised Ivy is heading back down south. There'll be a huge market for it in Glastonbury and she's assured of a workspace, thanks to Gideon.'

'Gideon?' The word was out before he could stop himself. 'Who's Gideon?'

'One of her friends.' Angel looked up

at Zac and, despite the times he had seen her bare-faced, he was once again briefly startled to see her without her customary make-up. Her clear skin was creamy and her eyes, although very dark and fringed with black lashes, which he knew she had tinted regularly, were bigger somehow without the sharp lines of kohl around them. She looked about fourteen. 'The friend who got her the workspace. *Gideon*.'

'Oh. That's nice,' Zac said. 'Gideon. Well, she could use my workshop. She only has to say.' He flapped his hand around in the general direction of the workshop. 'It's big enough for both of us. Are you going to tell me what happened with Kyle?'

'Nope,' replied Angel. She turned her head back to the magazine and flicked over a page. 'I take it he's not with you anyway. That's good. And there's a letter for you. She said you knew about it.' Angel did a good imitation of Zac's flapping hand, only she flapped hers in the direction of the coffee table.

'Ah yes. Ivy told me, and the solicitor mentioned something was on its way to me. This'll be it.' He leaned over to get it and looked sharply at Angel who was still studying the magazine, her face impassive. 'Don't think I'm letting you off with an explanation, no matter how exciting this letter might be,' he warned her. 'Although I doubt it's another property I've inherited as I might have known about that before now.'

Angel shrugged and flicked another page over, without looking at him. 'I doubt it will be exciting,' she commented. 'Probably dull as dishwater, especially if it concerns anything about your horrible cousin.'

Zac shook his head and turned his attention to the letter. It was a big, stiff white envelope, backed with cardboard — the sort that certificates and things came in that needed to stay flat. It was rather light and he weighed it in his hands before he opened it. 'It'll probably just be a bill or something, the guy I spoke to didn't elaborate,' he said and tore it open.

Zac peered in and saw a white sheet of paper and a smaller, rectangular envelope inside. Easing his fingers into the big envelope, he pulled the items out. The white sheet was a letter.

Dear Zac, the letter started, *Please find enclosed an envelope and accept our deepest apologies. These items were to be sent on to you under separate cover, as specified within Jeanie's Last Will and Testament, and it has come to our attention that the items were overlooked . . .*

The rest of the letter was legalese, referring to the Taigh Fallon and further instructions blah blah blah. Zac didn't take any of it in. He picked up the small envelope and frowned.

'Well open it!' Angel was watching him, the magazine abandoned on the floor beside her.

'Give me a moment!' he said, and ripped the top of that one too. Inside, was a folded note and a photograph of a young woman standing beside a huge plant. The woman was staring off into the distance looking confident and sure of herself, a smile on her lips.

'Who is she?' Angel was next to him, leaning over him, studying the photograph. 'She's very beautiful. Is that Jeanie?'

Zac shook his head. 'I don't think so. The clothing looks a bit too Victorian for her. Hang on.' He unfolded the smaller note and read it. 'Good Lord.' He re-read it, and read it again, just to make sure. 'Well. It isn't Jeanie. It's her grandmother, Annis.' He handed the letter over to Angel.

Angel's gaze roved over the letter and Zac had the satisfaction of seeing her eyes open wide and the colour drain from her face.

'Good Lord indeed, Zac. Your Great Aunt Jeanie thinks the place is haunted at any rate!' She sat down, cross-legged, right in the middle of the floor.

Dearest Zachary,
I trust I find you well. You will

273

inherit Taigh Fallon alongside any other young family members, and I anticipate young Kyle will be around at some point as well. But as you are the one who I suspect lives closest to the property, I find it my decision to entrust this to you. This photograph was the treasured possession of my Great Uncle Alasdair, who brought my father up as his own boy. The woman in the picture is my grandmother, Annis Jeanie Fallon, who was married to Alasdair's brother, Connor. Connor passed before my father was born, and Annis died very soon afterwards, drowned in the Loch, poor wee soul. My father was therefore orphaned at a few days old. I sometimes think their shades linger within that old house, then I put that down to the fancies of an old lady who wouldn't mind lingering there herself once she's passed! But don't worry — I shall not haunt you outright, my dear boy! Remember

*though, that Taigh Fallon knows
what is best for all who love it. It
will tell you all its secrets if you just
let it in.*

*Yours most sincerely,
Jeanie.*

The photograph was lying on the table
and Angel's eyes kept sliding over to it.
There was something about that lady
she found fascinating.

'Oh for goodness sake!' cried Zac eventually. 'Stop looking at that picture so
slyly. Here!' He leaned over and picked
it up, dropping it neatly into Angel's
lap. 'I can tell you're thinking all sorts of
things that I don't think I want to know.
Take it. Take it for a walk somewhere so
you can meditate on it or whatever you
want to do. Only bring it back safely.'

Angel's fingers closed around the
picture and she smiled at Zac. 'Thank
you Zac. I love you Zac.' She stood up.
'I think I'll go for a walk.'

'Go,' he said, almost with a snarl. 'Go
and meditate.'

The snarl reminded her uncomfortably of Kyle — only Kyle did it so much better . . .

26

Angel did indeed go for a walk, and she aimed for the derelict croft. Eventually, she sat down, feeling the cold, lumpy surface of the stone wall through the thin fabric of her nightgown and robe. It was fortunate, she thought wryly, that she had thought to throw one of Zac's jerseys on as well, as it was certainly not as warm as it had looked. But nevertheless, she took a deep breath, filling her lungs with the clear Skye air, a tang of salt clinging to the edges of it.

Annis. Annis Jeanie Fallon. *Taigh Fallon knows what is best for all who love it. It will tell you all its secrets if you just let it in.*

Very interesting. 'But what on earth can she mean?' Angel asked the photograph. She stared at the girl in the picture and studied her. She squinted her eyes and turned the photo this way and that, trying to recall everything she had experienced in the old house; trying to decide whether the shade of Annis had made itself known to her or not. Jeanie seemed convinced she was still at Taigh Fallon, anyway. But all Angel could really think about, though, was Kyle Fallon's dark eyes and semi-shaved state. In fact, if she closed her eyes completely, his image filled her mind. His smell, his energy, his voice . . .

She snapped her eyes open again. She didn't want to go down that route. She took hold of the picture in both hands and tried again.

Voices. She had heard voices in the tower room. She had felt fabric brushing past her as something hurried down the corridor. She traced the outline of the girl's dress. That was long enough to rustle and brush past people.

Ugh. Was this a route she definitely wanted to go down? Ghosts and old occupants of that house rushing around and arguing?

She remembered the baby crying. *Connor passed before my father was born, and Annis died very soon afterwards.*

'Oh my.' Angel suddenly felt faint. 'Was that little Connor I heard?' she asked, looking down at Annis. 'Your Connor. Your little boy?'

A feeling of overwhelming sadness passed over her and she shivered. Whether it was the thought of dying and leaving behind a newborn that had made her feel sad, or whether it was something else, she didn't know. She gripped the corners of the picture more tightly, conscious that her palms were sweating and hoping that the corners of the picture wouldn't curl up and get damaged.

Orphaned.

Poor little Connor didn't have a father either. The image of the mourning dress in her workshop laid heavily on her. Annis might have worn something like that. And if she had been in mourning, in that era —

'Of course!'

When the tower room had shifted, slipped back into Victorian times for that brief moment; when she had seen the bulky shape of the woman with the moonlight breaking through her hair. She had only seen the profile for a split second, but now it was as if someone had whispered the name into her mind. *Annis Jeanie Fallon.*

The candles, the slips of paper on the table — Angel knew enough about the Victorian era to know that séances had happened. Why on earth hadn't she realised before? That scene had been Annis trying to contact a loved one. Maybe the baby's father? The notes had been letters. It had been a makeshift Ouija board. Angel shuddered, fearfully this time. Despite the way she looked, Angel knew some things just shouldn't be messed with. Ouija boards were one of them. God knew what could happen if you opened portals with those things.

The very least of the user's problems would be hauntings. The very worst, demons. Perhaps they could even cause rifts in time — perhaps when she had been in that room, looking at the man before her, he knew her as well. Only as a shadowy person, a figure from —

The mirror.

A voice spoke in her ear. A gust of wind whipped up from nowhere and sighed past her, swirling into a grey mist beyond the rocks, dissipating into nothing.

Angel had had enough. She stood up, too quickly. A star was pricking through the darkening sky. A constant star. The same star that no doubt Annis and Alasdair and Jeanie and all the rest of them had looked at so many years ago.

Angel felt very small and very insignificant. She hitched up her skirt and ran for the croft as if the hounds of hell were chasing her.

*   *   *

Zac looked up from Angel's fashion magazine, startled, as she burst through the door. 'Angel Tempest! Talk about being named appropriately. You're like a whirlwind, coming in there. And that's my sweater, I believe.'

Angel just shook her head. 'I know who Annis is.'

'Yes. She's Jeanie's granny. We've established that,' replied Zac. 'You sure you're okay?'

'I'm fine. I've got to leave. I have to go home.'

'Yes. You planned to do that soon anyway.'

'I know. But it's just . . . *safer* at home. In Whitby. In Goth Cottage.' She shuddered. 'I'm just happier with my own ghosts, that's all. They don't bother me.'

'They don't bother you because your cottage isn't haunted!' said Zac with a laugh. 'It's just an old, creaky cottage that's got as much character as its owner. It's as haunted as this place.'

'Zac, anywhere people have lived and died is haunted. I thought you *knew* that. But your ghosts,' her voice caught on a sob, which astonished her, '*your* ghosts from Taigh Fallon. They've followed me here. I swear, someone talked to me out there and I think I saw something whoosh past me. The same voices must have been talking to Jeanie.'

'What voices?' Zac was genuinely stunned.

'The baby. The baby crying in the tower room and the talking and the rushing.' She mimicked a person running past her. 'The rushing past. That corridor. The mirror!'

'I think I'm missing something here.' Zac was confused, now.

'The reason we argued, me and Kyle, it was because he found me in the corridor. And there was something down there with me. I thought it was him, but it wasn't. And then I saw Kyle, properly. And there was something that I saw in the Loch as well, and Annis *drowned*, remember.' Angel clamped her lips shut, aware of the rising note of hysteria.

'Good grief, have you been at the whisky?' Zac asked, his eyes wide.

'Ghosts? The house was fine, nothing to fret over.'

'The house was wonderful. I loved it. I loved it from the moment I saw it. I felt I belonged there. What if it knew I was coming *back*?' Angel started to shake, her mind jumping illogically around. 'We were all in the room together. The tower room. And she'd done a séance. What if he saw me, the same way I saw him? What if we had met before?'

'Angel, darling, you're quite mad.' Zac shook his head. 'Seriously, if you haven't had some whisky, you need some.' He opened the bottle they had begun a few days ago, the first night she had stayed there, and poured double measures out for them both.

'I might be quite mad,' she replied, holding her hand out for the glass he proffered, 'but I just don't think Taigh Fallon has finished with me yet. Not if Jeanie is right. And it's beginning to get to me. I don't know what it's got planned for me. So maybe I'm running away.'

She sat down on the window seat and stared out over the water, as if that was her last word on it.

'Maybe it hasn't finished with you,' said Zac. 'Maybe it'll call you back somehow and you can sort things out. It seems like you've got unfinished business, whichever way you look at it. But running won't help. You can't run from Kyle and you can't run from your feelings.' He picked the magazine up, concentrating on, she assumed, the new fashions for his jewellery.

She was furious. 'My feelings?' Angel swivelled in her chair and stared at him. '*Feelings?* Good grief, Zac.'

And that, indeed, was Angel's last word on the subject. She didn't even want to consider a future intertwined with Taigh Fallon and Kyle; *because*, a small voice said in her head, *that really was too much to hope for*.

'What on earth have you against him?' cried Zac, tossing the magazine to the floor. 'I know you didn't get off to the most auspicious of starts, what with nearly pushing him down the stairs and all — but seriously, Ange, what the *hell* is your problem?'

'My problem is *you*, to be honest.' Okay, perhaps she had more words to say after all. 'Jeanie left you both that house. She wanted you both to do the very best possible for it. I heard what he was saying. I know what he does for a living.'

'Aye. He works in property development. What's wrong with that? It's a creative industry. You should have much in common.'

'I don't raze beautiful old buildings like Taigh Fallon to the ground. I don't decide that because one part of one corridor has a slightly dodgy floorboard that the whole house is unstable and needs to come down. Because of the land. Oh yes. The land. That's the part he wants, isn't it?' She slugged the measure of whisky back and poured herself another.

'The *land*?' Zac looked seriously confused now. 'He's never mentioned doing anything with the land at Taigh Fallon. He wants to restore it and make it safe for the next owner, because, yes, it *is* unsafe and I *won't* be keeping it. But we both need to agree what happens with it.'

'He definitely said something about using the land. I heard him quite clearly.'

Zac stared at her, frowning. She could almost hear the cogs turning in his head.

Then he opened his eyes wide and nodded. 'Aye. Come with me. I want to show you something.'

'No. I don't need to see anything.' She looked at the whisky in the glass and contemplated a third one. God, she would be hammered if she drank any more.

'You do. It's non-negotiable. Come on.' Zac stood up and his shadow fell across her. He held his hand out and she glowered at him. 'Give me that glass. Now, please.'

She toyed with the options for a moment, then reluctantly handed the glass over. 'Where are we going?' she asked miserably.

'We're going to where Kyle negotiated the land deal,' replied Zac shortly. He put the glass on the table and stared at her, his eyes as hard as the Cairngorm gems he worked with.

Angel clamped her lips together and put her hand in Zac's — resistance was, clearly, futile.

He hauled her to her feet. 'You might want your boots.' His voice was rather cold.

'Okay,' she replied flatly. Angel, as always, knew when she was beaten. It just didn't usually happen that Zac beat her.

She allowed him to lead her to the hallway and she put her boots on, consciously not catching Zac's eye. She was beginning to feel rather foolish and it pained her.

'Good. Now. Let's go,' said Zac.

This time he didn't take her hand. She followed him outside and he stormed ahead of her, in the direction of the ruined buildings she had sat on earlier.

'Oh no,' she whispered, suddenly understanding. 'Oh no.'

'Oh yes,' replied Zac.

'But where are we going?'

'I think you know.' Zac paused on the moors, letting her catch up. It was that weird time of day the Scots call the gloaming. The stars were peeking through the dusk, brighter now than before, but there was an otherworldly purple haze to the world. Rising up out of the fields, the bulky shape of the ruined croft greeted her in silence, squat under the stars. It made her shiver.

'This, my dearest Angel, is the piece of land my cousin is interested in developing,' said Zac, halting before the croft. 'This place needs to be condemned. Every time we have another storm or another blizzard, a bit more breaks off it, or another beam falls to the floor. The thing is rotten. It's dangerous.

'I told him all about it when I realised what he did. Asked if he had any suggestions as to what I could do about it. So he's going to look at it, and see what *he* can do. He'll either restore it or pull it down. And if he pulls it down, he'll be rebuilding it with as many of the original materials as he can. He's told me about his plans. He's going to develop a Folk Museum on the site, employ local people, give something back to the community. I said I'd help. Since he came back to Scotland and saw Taigh Fallon again, he's realised exactly what he's missed all these years. And he decided he wanted to put more of his heart and soul into the place. You know he was named for the Kyle of Lochalsh? Because that's where he was born? No? Aye, I guessed as much. You did nothing but argue with him, you made no attempt to get along with him. It wasn't the most comfortable of experiences for anyone involved. And good luck to him for wanting to do something with this wreck of a building. And, for what it matters, Taigh Fallon is safe.' He turned to her and shook his head despairingly.

'If you didn't jump to conclusions, life would be so much simpler.'

It was possibly the longest speech Angel had ever heard Zac make. 'Well what was I supposed to think? I never thought of this place.' Her voice was small and she felt a little silly.

'No, you wouldn't have done — because you only wanted to think the worst of Kyle. I really do despair of you. He's not half as bad as you wanted to believe.'

Angel looked at the ruins. In a strange way, she loved them as they were. She loved the fact that families had walked on those stone-flagged floors and maybe had some animals grazing outside the place. She liked to think of a gaggle of children, snuggled up together in a bed, tucked in with a rough, scratchy blanket around their chins — but the sensible side of her knew that the croft was genuinely just a pile of tumbledown stones and they needed a hell of a lot of work on them.

And if Kyle Fallon was willing to

pour his heart and soul into undoing some of the work of the Highland Clearances, then hats off to him.

She just wished she had known it sooner — before it was too late.

'I'm sorry,' she said, contrite. Her hand sought Zac's, hoping for a reassuring squeeze. He'd rarely exploded at her before and she felt awful. She also felt awful for Kyle. His face floated into her mind; that funny little half-smile, that frown that furrowed his brows. His energy his heat, his barely concealed passion. And her desire for him. She felt a little light-headed and a lot foolish. 'I'm sorry,' she said again.

'Maybe it's not me you need to apologise to,' said Zac quietly. But at least she was gratified to feel his hand squeeze hers in return — albeit after a little pause.

27

'Why? Why Angel? Why do you always have to call me at mega-inappropriate times?'

Jessie was moaning. Angel brushed it off. 'Do you have a man in bed with you?' she asked tartly. 'Am I interrupting anything?'

'I do not have a man with me. I was asleep, for God's sake!' snapped Jessie. 'I need my sleep. You *know* that. Why don't you ring Rosa? Rosa can help. Rosa is sensible.'

'Rosa talks to me like I'm a child, and you listen better.'

'What do I need to listen to at eleven o'clock at night?'

Angel heard Jessie shift in bed and a *thud* as something apparently fell onto the floor. Jessie swore. It would be a book then; Jessie had an enormous number of books and even as a child had fallen asleep reading them. Rosa maintained that Jessie still had a copy of Rosa's precious *Green Smoke* hidden somewhere inaccessible; a fact which Jessie strenuously denied.

'I might have made the worst decision in history.' Angel sighed. She sat, tonight, on the decking below the sun room at the croft. It was cool and still, the waves on the Sound of Sleat soothing as she curled up under her favourite patchwork blanket and stared over the water. There were lights bobbing around — maybe from boats, or maybe vehicles from distant shores — and she wondered if anybody was out there watching her light shining at the croft.

More specifically, she wondered if Kyle was sitting somewhere thinking of her. She doubted it.

'Dearest Angel. Whatever decision you have made is hardly going to be the worst in history.'

Angel scowled at the phone. Her sister's smooth contempt was irritating.

Jessie had always told her she was the Mistress of Hyperbole.

'Okay. Maybe not the worst in history,' she conceded, 'but I think I've pretty much screwed over my chances with someone.'

'Someone?' Jessie perked up. 'Kyle, perchance?'

Angel closed her eyes and dropped her head. 'Yes. Kyle.'

'Why?' Jessie was straight to the point.

'He's seemingly not as vile as I thought,' admitted Angel. She opened her eyes and looked up again, staring into the darkness. 'In fact he's doing quite a sweet thing for Zac and for the island.'

'Sweet?' Angel could almost see Jessie shaking her head. 'You don't need 'sweet'. It's like Rosa told you. You don't need another Zac.'

'No, and he's *not* another Zac. He's different. Do you know what?' She laughed, briefly. 'I actually miss him. I miss the arguing. I never thought I'd say that. I've known him less than a week, but it's like I want him here;

telling me off. Why? Why is that?'

'Because it's like a passion,' said Jessie. 'Like *Wuthering Heights*. Heathcliff is a beast to everyone except Cathy, really, but Cathy just *gets* him. She's the same as Heathcliff — it's no good with Edgar as he's too nice to her. She wants that Heathcliff passion.'

'Heathcliff was a holy terror,' said Angel. 'He was a rotter. I'd rather have Mr Darcy.'

'Yes, darling, wouldn't we all? But to return to my analogy, Zac's your Edgar and Kyle's your Heathcliff. It would never be dull.'

'I love Zac. He's like a brother. Edgar was pathetic.'

'That's as maybe. But of the two of them . . . Edgar or Heathcliff? Zac or Kyle?'

'Zac and I will never be more than friends.'

'That's not an answer.'

'Zac has to find a nice girl.'

'Still not an answer.'

A pause.

'Is it perhaps too much to say that I might have, only very slightly, started to change my mind about Kyle?' Angel squeezed her eyes shut again, waiting for the sarcastic tirade she expected from her sister. 'I want to see if anything — better — can happen. I think I want that chance. I want to see if it'll — work — better. You know? I don't want to wait until we're both dead and our ghosts are haunting the damn moors looking for each other. Having said that, I think he'd be glad to see me six feet under.'

Instead of the tirade, there was a soft chuckle at the end of the line. 'Ahh, Heathcliff and Cathy. You gotta love them. But only you can decide what you should do, darling. Now. I must go. I need to sleep. See you soon?'

'Yes. I'll see you soon. Thanks, honey.'

'You're very welcome, sweetie. Goodnight.'

'Goodnight.'

Jessie blew a little kiss down the line and Angel blew one back, then the line disconnected and there was just the soft hum of the dialling tone left.

Only you can decide what you should do.

It was easier said than done. She knew what her head was telling her, but her stubborn heart was telling her something completely different.

28

Zac prepared to wave Angel off the next day. She still looked a little like a rabbit caught in headlights, her face a little paler under the make-up than it had been, her eyes a little more shadowed.

'Am I forgiven?' he asked as he helped her with her luggage, and tucked it in the boot of her car.

'Forgiven for what?'

'For suggesting that deep down you might not want to murder my cousin?'

She smiled, and he smiled back, relieved. Angel was his best friend and he hated to think of them parting on a bad note.

'You're forgiven. So long as I am. Murder might not be top of my list for him, but he's ridiculously annoying, you've got to grant me that. It's just as well you don't share that part of your genetics, isn't it, otherwise I couldn't love you best of all.'

Zac laughed and hugged her. 'It's been so nice to see you. It's my turn to come to Whitby next.'

'Hmm.' Angel raised her eyebrows. 'We both know that's not likely to happen. Zachary Fallon on the mainland? God forbid. But you know, The Room has space for an airbed if you do come, so don't let that put you off.'

'Aye.' He was non-committal.

Angel shook her head and gave him one last hug before she slid into her car. 'Well, I have a long drive, so I'm off.'

'No stopover in Edinburgh?'

'No stopover. I just want to get back. You know?' A shadow flickered across her face and Zac nodded. He understood, somehow, that she had a few things to settle in her mind and, for Angel, a long drive was probably as good a place as any to do it.

'Okay, call me en route. Let me know you're safe.'

'Will do.' She shut the door and blew him a kiss. The car pulled away and he stood at the end of the track waving to her until the car was a dot.

He turned and headed towards the workshop, thinking about the next piece of jewellery he was going to make. He had some amethyst which would be quite nice set into a Celtic cross and —

'I like Angel.'

He looked up and saw Ivy standing at the door of the tea room. She must have been there to see her off as well, perhaps waving the tartan tea-towel she was now twisting into a sausage shape between her long, pale fingers.

Zac smiled. 'Yes, she's a good friend,' he said. 'I'm pleased you liked her. Next time she comes up, you'll have to take her to the village. I'm sure she'd like that — more exciting than being here for her, I suppose. But she had Taigh Fallon to think about this time, so you didn't get a chance to see more of her. I'm sorry.'

Ivy shrugged. 'Don't be sorry. We've exchanged numbers and things. She said I'd probably enjoy Whitby. Do you know, I've never been.' She gazed out at the little track that led away from the croft. 'I'll call in on my way to Glastonbury if I can. Break my journey.'

'What?' Zac stopped and stared at her. 'Glastonbury? You mean it?'

'Aye.' She began to twist the tea-towel the other way and then shook it out angrily. 'I *am* going, Zac. I've told you several times and I'm not changing my mind. Do I have to hand an official letter in? And how much notice do I have to give?'

'I don't want to accept your notice or your letter. I don't want you heading to Glasto with Gideon. He's a hairy beast adorned in hemp and smelling of patchouli.'

Ivy suddenly laughed. 'No, he's not.' She studied Zac for a moment and smiled, her voice softening. 'Maybe it won't be forever, Zac. Maybe I just have to do this. Just to try it. I might yet come back.'

'Hmm.' Zac stared at her, a curious

mix of feelings surging around his mind. 'I'll miss you.'

'And I'll miss you. But we'll survive.' She flicked the end of the tea-towel at him and grinned. 'Come on. Let's have a coffee and talk about what you want in an assistant.'

She turned and headed into the tea room. Zac simply stared after her. There was only one thought he could come up in response to that: *You. I want* you.

29

1897

It was a week or two after Annis's death and Alasdair was sitting in the tiny, darkened hallway at the bottom of the spiral staircase. He had taken to going there with a bottle of whisky and his thoughts at odd times of the day and night, and tonight he had brought three extra things with him.

One of the items was a photograph of Annis — posed by a huge plant, she stared off into the distance looking confident and happy. It had been taken before she had become engaged to Connor and she was clear-eyed and untainted by all that was to come afterwards. It was Alasdair's favourite picture of her. Someone, he didn't know who, had suggested they call in a photographer to capture Annis after the drowning and place baby Connor next to his dead mother for posterity, thanks to a hideous new fashion that folk with a fascination for death had begun — the creation of a memento mori.

Alasdair had raged at everyone and refused point blank to entertain the idea. Why would he want to be reminded of her like that, when he had this beautiful picture of her? The thought sickened him. He knew, also, that he would never forget her floating in the Loch and the image was seared into his mind as it was. That was the reason for the whisky. Sometimes, it made him sleep.

The second item was the sketch of the angel Annis had summoned during those awful séances. That dark beauty hadn't helped in the end. Alasdair's prayers had been answered, after a fashion, and they had both survived the birth as he wished. He wished now, though, that he had been more specific. He had tried to deny it, but that angel had been an angel of death. He ought to have known something like this was coming when she had first appeared. But he had blanked it out, damped the feeling down because she was beautiful and fascinating, and he was loathe to believe she could bring any harm to them.

But séances were new and demons had been around for eternity. He studied the sketch. He still found it difficult to believe she was evil. He still refused to believe it. The love he felt for Annis was a strange, watered down version of the pull he felt to this creature. It made him feel guilty as sin, as if he was denying the purity of whatever he felt for Annis. Yet it was not a pure love, was it, with Annis? It never had been. It was sinful; it was lust. It was the desire for his brother's wife. He groaned and folded the paper up, not wanting to pursue the matter any further.

The third item was the angel's ring. The jet ring with the diamond flower on it. For that, he had no explanation. He glanced up at the mirror, fancying *he could see her shadow there; but it was empty.*

He lined the three items up on his lap. The photograph would stay with him, come what may. The sketch and the ring — he did not want them found. He wanted them hidden away.

And he wanted the angel even more than he wanted Annis. He thought he might want her forever.

★ ★ ★

About four weeks after his return from Taigh Fallon, Zac was missing Ivy McFarlane more than he thought possible. He was losing himself in the workshop, trying not to think about her, and leaving the running of the tea room to Effie, another lady from the village who had swept in and taken over very efficiently.

He looked up from the piece of stone he was fixing into a necklace, startled out of his glooming by a loud car engine and the crunch of gravel as the vehicle jammed its brakes on. A clash of the car door, and a shadow passed over the window as the owner strode purposefully past the workshop.

Then the door of the workshop flung open. 'Hey. I'm glad I found you. It's kinda important.' Kyle was standing there in front of him, then his cousin shoved his hands in his pockets and scowled. 'I know I've kind of sprung this visit on you, but there are some things I need to get straight in my head. You're the best person to help me.'

'Kyle! Good to see you. Is it about that ruin? Do you need anything for it? Sorry — not sure if you need to survey the land first or something.' Zac looked around vaguely as if someone other than Kyle would appear to answer that question, but of course they didn't. He was no good with this sort of stuff. Ivy would have known, he was pretty sure about that. Damn the fact she was in bloody Glasto.

Kyle's lip twitched into his almost-smile. 'Cool. Yeah, I'll take a look. That was part of it. But there was something else I needed to ask you. The surveying could wait. This couldn't.'

'Whatever you need.' Zac opened his eyes wide in surprise. 'But I don't know what could be so urgent for you.'

Kyle's lips twitched again, stretched a little further into a rueful smile. 'Oh believe me. There's something pretty damn urgent.'

'Come on then. We'll walk to the ruins and you can tell me on the way. D'you want a coffee? Tea? We can do a takeaway, carry it with us?'

Kyle paused. 'Yeah. We can do a takeaway.'

Zac smiled at his cousin again. 'Come on then. Let's get the drinks from Effie and you can tell me what it is that's bothering you.'

30

'So are you *sure* you didn't see any ghosts then?'

Grace Eleanor Nelson had obviously been desperate to find that out. She had wandered into Angel's open shop as soon as the opportunity had arisen. But between school and parties and dancing classes and Charlie and Aunt Lissy visiting, she hadn't managed to talk to Angel properly, at length, about it. But now, she clearly had a break in her busy schedule. Angel had propped the door open to let some fresh May air dance around the little room, as the weather was getting warmer and the workshop was becoming stuffy. Grace had clearly seen this as an open invitation.

'No darling, like I told you, I didn't.' Angel smiled at the little girl. She must have been working on her mum, or, more likely, her Aunt Lissy had disregarded Becky's wishes, as today her nails were black with tiny sparkles in the polish.

'Oh that's a shame.' Grace frowned. 'I'm sorry I haven't had more time to come to your workshop, Angel. We were in London where Aunt Cori lives last weekend. Kitty is *too* much. She's worse than Charlie.' Grace rolled her eyes, looking and sounding exactly like her Aunt Lissy in miniature. Kitty, from what Angel had gathered, was a toddler cousin of sorts and was acceptable in small doses. 'I thought you might have seen something scary on your holidays. I thought you might like to talk properly about it. Now I'm back.'

Angel's mind flashed over an image of Kyle Fallon; dark, brooding and Heathcliff-like in his tempers. 'There was a man,' she said, 'who was a little bit scary until I got to know him. Then he wasn't so scary after all.' She remembered the kiss they'd shared and the heat rushed up through her body again.

'And will he be coming to Whitby?' Everything was so clear-cut to Grace. Whitby was the centre of the universe to her and, as far as she was concerned, every man and his dog should gravitate there at least once.

'I doubt that. He lives in Canada so I probably won't see him again.'

'But Aunt Lissy and Uncle Stef live in Italy sometimes, and I still see them.' It was the voice of reason from a six year old.

'Yes, but they love you very much and like to come to see you.'

'The man might love *you* very much. What's his name?'

'It's Kyle. And I don't think he loves me at all. Now, I have to get this little ring done, so would you like to help me polish up the jet a bit more? I don't think it's quite shiny enough yet, do you?'

Grace shook her head. 'No, Angel. It's not. I can make it better for you.' She clambered up to the workbench and slid into place next to Angel.

'Good girl.' Angel bunked along to let the child help. She passed her the gem and a chamois leather and Grace began industriously rubbing the jet, her bottom lip caught between her teeth as she concentrated on it.

Eventually, Grace held the stone up to the light and half-closed her eyes as she had seen Angel do a hundred times. 'What's the ring going to look like?'

'Like the one I lost. It fell off my finger when I was in Scotland. I never found it. It had a little flower on it, made of diamonds. You would have loved it. Look, try rubbing that bit there a little more — super.'

'I think it needs to look a little like this one.'

The voice was unmistakeable and Angel snapped her head up.

He was standing in front of the table, holding a silver-set ring in the palm of his hand; it looked tiny, huddled there apologetically.

'I found it by accident,' he said, almost conversationally. Angel couldn't take her eyes off him. He kept his gaze fixed on the ring and tilted his hand so it slid off and landed on the desk with a little tinkle.

'Oh that is *very* pretty.' Grace's oddly coloured eyes lit up.

'Yes, isn't it?' He turned his attention to the little girl. 'And you are?'

'I'm Grace. My daddy has the photograph studio.' She pointed outside. 'I'm helping Angel today.'

'And you're doing a fine job,' he said.

'Thank you,' she replied graciously.

Angel remained speechless. She cleared her throat and shifted position a little.

The man smiled at the little girl. 'Did you draw that picture up there?' He nodded at a picture of a raven-haired princess in a tower. It was meant to be Rapunzel, but was clearly the Goth version of Rapunzel. It was largely drawn in black felt tip and the princess even had a tiny black stud in her nose. Angel had loved it and subsequently pinned it up behind her workspace.

'Yes. It's a princess,' replied Grace.

314

'It's quite a good picture, I think.'

'It's a very good picture, and it even reminds me of a story. Would you like to know where exactly I found this pretty little ring?'

Grace nodded avariciously, staring at the piece of jewellery.

'Well, it's an extraordinary story. I was staying in a very old house and there was a secret corridor. And that corridor led down a big staircase from a tower room out onto the beach. Isn't that exciting?'

'Ooh.' Grace's eyes widened.

'And between the big old house and the secret door to the beach was a room. Not a very big room; but big enough. And in that room, was a vase. Now, the vase was very old. And one day, the vase had a bit of an accident.'

'How? How did it have an accident?' Grace was clearly caught up in the story, his hypnotic Canadian voice working its magic on his young audience.

'The vase fell. Okay, I say it fell, when what I *may* mean was that it was picked up and thrown against a wall.'

'*Thrown*?' Grace was entranced.

'Uh-huh. Thrown. By a man with a really, really bad temper. That's terrible, isn't it?'

Grace nodded. 'Terrible.'

'He had a bad temper because the princess who used to stay in the tower had gone away and she hadn't said goodbye to him. And he was sad.'

'Was the man a prince?' Grace had kneeled up on the seat and was leaning on the bench, her eyes like saucers, the jet ring she was making forgotten. Mechanically, Angel moved the cloth and the gem out of her way, just in case.

'No. He wasn't a prince. But if he was a prince, he would have known exactly what to say to the princess. But instead, they just argued. And they argued so much, she left. And then he broke the vase. And the ring was hidden in the vase. Now, nobody knows who put it in there, but I think it might have been there for a very long time. Or *not* a very long time at all. Because the house was magical, you see, and the princess was magical and it was all very strange.'

'Ooh.'

'Exactly. 'Ooh'. And there was something else in the vase too. There was a picture. A picture someone had drawn, a very long time ago.'

'How did you know it was drawn a very long time ago?' asked Grace.

'Because the paper was so old and the ink was so faded. And the ring was wrapped up in the paper and you could just tell it was old and it was creased so much, it was almost torn in the creases.'

The man reached into his pocket and pulled out a small square of folded, yellowed paper. He held it up. 'What do you think this is, Grace-my-daddy-has-the-photograph-studio?'

Grace giggled. 'That's not my proper name! It's just Grace.'

'Ah!' said the man, nodding. 'It was a big name for a little girl, so I'm pleased about that. Okay, Just-Grace. What do you think it is?'

'Oh! Oh! I think it might be the *drawing*!' she said, breathlessly.

'Very good. It might be. Shall we see?'

Grace nodded and Kyle unfolded the paper carefully onto the desk. Grace leaned further across and peered over it, blocking Angel's vision.

'It is! It's a drawing! Look! Look Angel!' She sat back and pointed to the paper. 'See what it is? It's your roses!'

Angel smiled weakly at the child and reached a hand out tentatively to pull it towards her. There was beat. A rush of she didn't know what flooded through her body, from her feet, right up to her head. It left her shaking.

'Good grief!' Even her voice was unsteady. The drawing was a perfect copy of the tattoo on the inside of her wrist, surrounding a picture of her very own face, even down to the diamond stud in her nose.

'She looks like you, doesn't she?' asked Grace excitedly. 'Do you think it's the princess? The princess from the tower?'

Angel just shook her head. 'I don't know, sweetheart. I really don't.' She looked up and for the first time in what seemed like forever, her eyes met Kyle's and he was there in front of her, and she wasn't just dreaming about him in the early hours of the morning, or thinking about him when she couldn't sleep. He was there. In her shop. With the ring she'd lost and a sketch of her, done by someone, it seemed, a hundred years ago or more.

'Hmm. It's interesting, isn't it?' He fixed Angel with his gaze. 'Shall I see, Just-Grace, whether the roses look like Angel's or not?'

Grace shrieked with delight. 'You know her name!'

'It's above the door, isn't it?' Kyle said. 'It was very easy to find her. I got a little help from my cousin because he gave me that clue. Anyway. May I?' He reached out and his fingers brushed Angel's hand. She nodded dumbly as he pressed his fingers to her skin and turned her arm so that her inner wrist was facing upwards. The sparks ran up and down her body, her skin prickling with electricity.

He leaned in, bending over her arm, pretending to study the tattoo; in reality, Angel knew he was simply holding her hand and feeling the same connection she did.

'It looks very like it,' he said. Angel was aware of the undercurrent and prayed that Grace wouldn't pick anything up. 'It's very strange indeed.'

He stood up, but didn't leave go of her wrist. 'As I say, it was a very magical place. Strange things happened in there. In fact, do you know, I might even have fallen in love with that princess if I'd been given the chance. If I'd known her properly, that is.'

Angel found her voice again. 'But what if the princess lived a very long way away from you? I mean, I don't think you're from England, are you?'

He smiled, his dark eyes crinkling at the edges. It was possibly the first time she'd seen him properly smile, seen him let his guard down enough to do so. 'No. I'm from Canada. But as it happens, I've just bought a house. It's an old house and I had to negotiate with my cousin for it. But I love that house and I think my princess loves it too. So it's there and it's ready for her, if she ever wants to go there again. It's in Scotland, so it's hardly on the doorstep, but you know.' He shrugged. 'The opportunity is there. I'll be coming over as much as I can. I can work from anywhere, so long as I have internet and a few old condemned properties to play with.'

'Scotland!' Grace piped up. 'Isn't that where you've just been Angel?'

Angel nodded.

'Wouldn't it be lovely if you were the Scottish princess?' the little girl continued, 'and you could go to the old house with the corridor?'

'It would be,' said Angel, 'but I've got a business to run.'

'You get time off, though, I'm sure. The house is big enough to make one of the rooms into a workshop. Eventually, there might be scope to employ an assistant so you could spend a bit more time up there.' Kyle shrugged. 'I'm thinking ahead. A lot ahead. All I'm thinking of really, right now, is the fact that I miss my princess and I want to spend some time with *her* — without the arguments, and without the shouting.' He looked at the ring on the workbench. 'It seems to me that she was meant to be there, at that big house, some way or another. Maybe she'd already been there? Who knows?'

'Maybe. I think she felt like that perhaps. But what about the man the princess saw in the mirror?' asked Angel. 'And the man in the tower room? Who was he?'

'I don't know,' said Kyle. 'The same as I don't know who the princess was that I saw. Shadows, maybe? Some sort of magic? Who knows what went on in that house so long ago? All I know, is that it felt like home. And I wanted my princess.'

'She wanted her prince as well,' replied Angel. 'But she didn't quite know how to get him.'

'I can probably advise on that,' he replied. He lifted her hand and pressed his lips to it, his eyes never leaving hers.

'I'd be interested to find out what you recommend,' said Angel.

'So did the prince and the princess fall in love and get married?' asked Grace, reminding them of her presence, still thinking about the fairy tale she had heard.

'I don't know yet,' said Kyle, 'but it'll be fun to find out.'

'Good.' Grace nodded and picked up the ring. She placed it in her own palm and stared at it thoughtfully. 'Because Angel doesn't do white, but she'd look lovely in a black wedding dress. And I'd be a very good bridesmaid.'

Epilogue

1903

Connor sat on his Uncle Alasdair's lap. At the grand old age of six, he chose not to do this when anybody else was at Taigh Fallon. But when they were together, in the big library near the warm kitchens, he would clamber up and listen to the stories his uncle would tell him.

Today, Connor held a little black ring carefully in his palm. It had sparkly, shiny diamonds on it, and they were in the shape of a flower. He rubbed at it, making it even more shiny and tilted his hand so the jewels caught the sunlight coming in through the window.

'Thank you for letting me hold your special ring,' he said to his uncle. 'Tell me the story about it again. Please?'

Uncle Alasdair looked down at him

and smiled. 'The story about the princess in the tower?'

'Aye! That one. Please.'

'Very well. Once upon a time, there was a princess.'

'Did she look like Mama?' Connor's eyes drifted over to the photograph of his mother his uncle always kept on his desk. She was very beautiful and smiled a lot in the photograph. His uncle told him she had smiled a lot when she was alive, and that she especially smiled at her husband, Connor's father, who had been a very brave and handsome man. Uncle Alasdair said that Connor looked like his father and Connor was pleased about that.

'No. She didn't look like your mama. The princess had very dark hair, as black as that ring you are holding so carefully for me, and she wore a beautiful black dress. And the prince was the only one who knew about her. Because, you see, she was trapped in a mirror, and the prince was the only one who could save her.'

'And how did he save her, Uncle Alasdair?'

'He saved her,' Uncle Alasdair said with a smile, 'because he loved her. And he always would. No matter how many years would pass. He would love his princess forever. And he knew that even in the future, when many, many years had passed, they would still find each other and love each other again. And it always seemed to the prince, no matter how far he travelled and how many lives he lived, that his princess was meant to be there, in the mirror, in that tower, in that house, in some way or another. And he knew they would always meet again.'

'It's a beautiful story, Uncle.' Connor smiled up at him. 'That's what princes and princesses do in fairy tales, isn't it? They fall in love.'

'Aye. But sometimes, just sometimes, it takes a little time. But they do, son, they always do fall in love — eventually.'

And little Connor very much hoped the story was true.

Thank You

Thank you so much for reading, and hopefully enjoying, Angel and Kyle's story — a stormy Scottish tale I loved writing. Angel needed someone she could unleash all that Gothic passion at, and I think Kyle does a pretty good job of being her Byronic hero. I hope you agree that he's a great match for her!

However, authors need to know they are doing the right thing, and keeping our readers happy is a huge part of the job. So it would be wonderful if you could find a moment just to write a quick review on Amazon or one of the other websites to let me know that you enjoyed the book. Thank you once again, and do feel free to contact me at any time on Facebook, Twitter, through my website or through my lovely publishers Choc Lit.

Thanks again, and much love to you all,
Kirsty
xx

We do hope that you have enjoyed reading this large print book.

Did you know that all of our titles are available for purchase?

We publish a wide range of high quality large print books including:
Romances, Mysteries, Classics
General Fiction
Non Fiction and Westerns

Special interest titles available in large print are:
The Little Oxford Dictionary
Music Book, Song Book
Hymn Book, Service Book

Also available from us courtesy of Oxford University Press:
Young Readers' Dictionary
(large print edition)
Young Readers' Thesaurus
(large print edition)

For further information or a free brochure, please contact us at:
Ulverscroft Large Print Books Ltd.,
The Green, Bradgate Road, Anstey,
Leicester, LE7 7FU, England.
Tel: (00 44) **0116 236 4325**
Fax: (00 44) **0116 234 0205**

A YEAR IN JAPAN

Patricia Keyson

When ex-librarian Emma announces she's accepted a year-long position to teach English in Japan, the news shocks her grown children. Enjoying single life after half a year of estrangement from her husband Neil, Emma can't wait to embark upon her adventure in three weeks. Then Neil is hospitalised after a car accident, and needs a carer at home while he recovers. Emma is the only one available to help. Three weeks — can Neil make up for lost time before Emma leaves, and will she let him back into her heart?

GRANDPA'S WISH

Sarah Swatridge

Melanie is growing tired of her job at a family law firm, until she is tasked with tracing a Mr Davies, the beneficiary of a late client's estate. Tracking him down, Melanie is surprised to find Robbie-Joe uninterested in the terms of the will, especially when he learns that it belonged to a grandfather he had no idea existed. To claim his fortune, Robbie-Joe must complete twelve challenges in twelve months. But Melanie has a challenge of her own: to stop her feelings for Robbie-Joe becoming anything more than professional . . .

HOME TO MISTY MOUNTAIN

Jilly Barry

UK-born Hayley Collins is visiting Australia, staying with a friend and looking for work. Craig Maxwell runs a holiday resort at Misty Mountain, a four-hour drive from Melbourne. When Hayley applies to be an administrator at the resort, Craig takes her on — and much else besides. She has to return to England in twelve months. He's engaged to a woman whose father is helping to keep the resort's finances in the black. so when Hayley and Craig fall in love, it seems a future together is only a distant dream . . .

RUBY LOVES . . .

Christina Garbutt

Crime writer Adam finds the peace he needs to finish his latest novel in a remote stately home in Carwyn Bay, Wales — at least until effervescent, disaster-prone Ruby arrives to run the tourist café while also pursuing a secret plan to uncover her grandfather's past. Through baking disasters and shocking revelations, they find themselves falling in love. But Ruby is saddened by what she learns about her grandfather, and plans to go home to America at the end of the summer. Will their relationship be strong enough to last?

ROMANCE AT THE CAT CAFÉ

Suzanne Ross Jones

Maxine Flynn leaves behind her unfulfilling accountancy job and unsupportive fiancé to live her dream of owning a cat café. Her beloved cats keep her company, so there's no room for romance — until she meets handsome next-door grocer Angus McRae, who conceals a warm heart under a gruff exterior. But with the grocery losing money and customers, and Maxine dealing with an unwelcome visitor from her past, plus mischievous lost cats, the road to romance isn't always a smooth one. Will they be able to make a future together?